POODLE'S GRAVE

Detective Sergeant Leonard Beckworth (retired) is asked by a neighbour to keep an eye on her house while she goes into hiding to dodge the publicity following her inheritance of a fortune in the USA. He obliges but when he finds the grave of her pet poodle in her back garden, Beckworth considers this utterly alien and inexplicable. With the help of a local newshound he makes enquiries . . .

Books by Howard Charles Davis
in the Linford Mystery Library:

DEATH IN THE SCILLIES
AND MURDER WON
DEAD MAN'S CROSS
POODLE'S GRAVE

HOWARD CHARLES DAVIS

POODLE'S GRAVE

Complete and Unabridged

LINFORD
Leicester

First published in Great Britain in 1981 by
Robert Hale Ltd.,
London

First Linford Edition
published November 1989

British Library CIP Data

Davis, Howard Charles
Poodle's grave.—Large print ed.—
Linford mystery library
I. Title
823'.914[F]

ISBN 0-7089-6750-7

Published by
F. A. Thorpe (Publishing) Ltd.
Anstey, Leicestershire
Set by Rowland Phototypesetting Ltd.
Bury St. Edmunds, Suffolk
Printed and bound in Great Britain by
T. J. Press (Padstow) Ltd., Padstow, Cornwall

Author's Note

MANY of the places named in this story are pure invention on my part but some actually exist. It would be as well, therefore, for me to point out that this is entirely a work of fiction and that any resemblance to a real person either living or dead portrayed by a character in this story is entirely coincidental.

1

DETECTIVE SERGEANT LEONARD BECKWORTH CID had been retired from No. 8 Regional Crime Squad for three months when his sister died. The event in itself, though he was shocked to learn of it if only because the death of a close relative always tends to remind a man of his own mortality, meant little to Beckworth. His sister Betty had been ten years older than he. He had not set eyes upon her for twenty-five years and that upon the occasion of her wedding to a marine engineer, to whom Beckworth had taken a dislike. Apart from the fact that his brother-in-law had been what Beckworth considered a bit of a Bible puncher he had also been a teetotaller . . . there had been nothing but a wishy-washy claret cup at the wedding . . . and this had damned the Chief Engineer in Beckworth's eyes for ever.

Over the years he had lost touch with his sister. Upon receiving news of her death he was surprised to learn that Arnold Timpson had predeceased his wife and that they had no children. He was even more surprised to learn that he had inherited the whole of his sister's estate which consisted after taxes of eight thousand pounds in a Building Society and a freehold property on the outskirts of a village called Funtingdon in West Sussex, named Splitlevel Cottage.

"Jesus!" Beckworth exclaimed when given the news by the representative of his sister's solicitors who had traced him through the medium of the Metropolitan Police. "Splitlevel Cottage? I bet the Chief Engineer thought that one up. Sure it's not Spiritlevel Cottage? And where the hell is Funtingdon?"

At first he was inclined to think that he would sell the cottage, lock, stock and barrel, for Beckworth was not and never had been a country man. But three months with nothing to do but amble down to the local and drink beer through

2

licensing hours was beginning to pall. Ever since the loss of his wife when both had been comparatively young Beckworth had been a drinker, albeit nearly always beer. There were many who said that his liking for drink had been responsible for his never having attained higher rank because it had made him careless in the way he addressed his superior officers, and downright diabolical in the way he had treated any villains unfortunate enough to cross his path. He had also grown scruffy in appearance with a huge paunch and a big flabby face. All the same quite a few of those who condemned his beer drinking were ready to admit that Leonard Beckworth had been a pretty good Jack.

But the ex-detective sergeant was beginning to wish that he had something to do in retirement, and he wondered if life in an entirely new environment might not provide an answer, or a job of some sort perhaps. He was only just fifty. In addition he had a feeling of guilt that he should have failed to communicate with his sister over such a number of years that on her death he had known literally nothing of her. In spite of this she had seen fit to bequeath him all she possessed and he thought that the least he could do was accept the gift of her home in the same spirit of loyalty with which it had obviously been made.

Enquiries concerning the location of Funtingdon brought the information that it was a village about three miles west of Chichester. Beckworth had recently been on a case that had required him to give evidence in the Crown Court at Chichester. He knew the way. He got out his old red Cortina and drove down there.

It was a very early spring morning, cold but sunny. The daffodil buds had assumed nodding angles and were beginning to show tips of yellow, not the least in the front garden of Splitlevel Cottage which had rank after rank of them bordering its short drive. The property was not a cottage at all but a modern bungalow of a squarish not unpleasing design set in half an acre of land carved out of a wheat field about half a mile out of the village. Its nearest neighbour looked to be a house shrouded in trees three hundred yards along the road to the village. Another gap then the cluster of houses, cottages and trees, not to mention the church, of the village itself where the road curved. Round the corner was a pub. Beckworth had checked on that and considered it to be within a not unreasonable distance.

He had been given the keys to the property by the solicitors concerned, who had told him at the same time that a Miss Tatchell, the nearest neighbour, had kindly consented to look in now and again to keep an eye on the place, for which she had been given a key.

The Chief Engineer, who had died a year before Betty, miserly though Beckworth had quite unjustly suspected him to be, had, he discovered, provided his wife with a sumptuous and comfortable home. The bungalow was richly furnished, not that Beckworth cared overmuch about the quality of its chairs or carpets, or the size of the bath. He was pleased to see that the large back garden, though mostly lawn, had a sizeable vegetable plot. He had always secretly envied those colleagues who had possessed gardens and grew vegetables. This garden, he saw, had a greenhouse and a big cold frame as well. He could find a new interest there. The gardening need not interfere with a job if he got one, nor his social life, which to begin with promised to be nothing but the daily visits to the local. But he could have a full life here.

The bungalow was in a spotless condition and he supposed that he ought really to call upon Miss Tatchell, who, if she were the nearest neighbour, must occupy the house amongst the trees, and thank her, but he decided it could wait till he had taken up residence. He called at the local instead where he found the three pints of beer he had with a cold lunch an excellent brew.

A week later he stuffed his few

possessions into the Cortina and left his North London bed-sitter for good. In later years the room had been costing him a comparative fortune in rent, and now, thanks to his sister Betty, all he would have to worry about would be the rates.

He had been at Funtingdon three days, and already the locals were saying, "Good morning" to his shambling figure, when busy clearing up in the kitchen after his breakfast he heard a dog yapping outside. A female voice shouted: "Shut up, Butch! You stupid animal." The dog's noise died to an eager whimper, he heard a key rattling in the front door, which was opened, and the same female voice called: "Hi! Anyone at home?"

Beckworth thought, "What the hell?" and went through into the hall. He saw a woman standing inside the front door with a white poodle on a red lead. As soon as it sighted Beckworth the dog began barking again; the noise agonizingly shrill within the confines of the house. Its owner yanked it upwards on the lead, put a beringed hand under it, clasped it to a

7

shapely bosom, and put her other hand round its jaws successfully silencing it.

"Bloody animal!" she exclaimed. "How d'yer do? I'm Tatch. You must be Betty Timpson's brother, Leonard. Sorry to barge in like this . . . first moment I've had. Good thing you weren't still in bed . . . what?"

Beckworth thought: "Oh, God." Aloud he mumbled a good morning.

"Well, aren't you the lucky bastard?" Miss Tatchell went on cheerfully. "Yer sister hadn't set eyes on you for twenty-five years and yet she's left you all she had. Can't be bad, can it? Still, I'm not the one to talk. I've got an old uncle lives in the States I've never set eyes on in me life, not even as a babe in arms. I heard the other year through my solicitors that the old idiot had made me his heir. How do you like that? Still, what the hell will I do with a chicken farm in Texas?"

Miss Tatchell laughed showing gleaming teeth. She was a strikingly handsome woman in immaculately tailored biscuit-coloured slacks and jersey of the

8

same colour. She was wearing a short musquash jacket against the outdoors and its big collar had been pulled up to frame her head. Maybe the glossy look of her dark hair owed much to the skill of her hairdresser but Beckworth guessed that in its natural state it would still be fine. With her Junoesque figure, her big beautiful brown eyes and generous mouth she reminded him of his long-dead wife, though Miss Tatchell was of course much older than his memory of Cynthia. How much older he couldn't guess. She must be in her late forties he supposed.

"I must admit I feel a bit guilty about it now," he said. "I mean getting out of touch with Betty. But you know how it is. They lived in Portsmouth at one time. I was moved around a lot as a youngster. The last letter I wrote came back, 'Not known at this address'." Beckworth paused awkwardly. He was twisting the teacloth he had forgotten to put down. He couldn't keep the woman standing in the hall. In spite of her colourful language she was obviously a lady.

"Care for a cup of coffee?" he found himself asking. "I was just going to make one for myself," he added, lying easily.

"Yes, why not? Thank you, Leonard. Don't mind me calling you Leonard, do you? Forgotten your surname. People call me Tatch. Me christian name's Tasmin. God-awful name it is too in my opinion. Let's have the coffee in the kitchen, eh? Butch can run in the back garden, if you don't mind."

"Sure. Odd name for a poodle, ain't it?"

He ushered her into the kitchen. Thank God, it was not in too bad a state of disarray.

"He inherited it," she replied. "I've always called my dogs Butch. Used to have Boxers at one time. I can't handle 'em so well now . . . too big. But the poodle's not a bad little chap though I curse him hard enough at times, don't I, Butch?"

She let the animal run trailing its scarlet lead as soon as she had opened the back door. Beckworth made the coffee and when they were seated at the kitchen table sipping the brew she said:

"My real reason for calling is to tell you about Mrs. Nash. She's the cleaning lady who's been looking in regularly keeping the place shipshape since Betty died. Thought you might still require her services. Heard you were a bachelor."

"Widower," Beckworth corrected her. "Yes. Thank you. I could do with some help in the house . . ."

"A pound an hour. I don't know how many she's put in already, but I'll tell her to come along and see you, and you can make your own arrangements . . ."

"And square up with her," Beckworth said.

The conversation turned to his sister then Miss Tatchell finished her coffee and stood up.

"Thanks a lot, Len. I'll go out the back way and collect the dog before he's piddled on the beetroot . . . what? Drop in on me any evening you feel like a drink. I'll be glad to see you. I'm in Orchard House up the road."

"Half a minute," Beckworth put in. "Orchard House. That rings a bell. I found a key in the kitchen drawer there with a label on it marked Orchard House."

"That's right. I let Betty have it for use in emergency. Better stick to it." Miss Tatchell put a scarlet-nailed finger under one eye. "See these big brown beautiful orbs? They're a snare and a delusion, Len. I've had cataracts removed from both and have to wear contact lenses. Without 'em I am as blind as the Sphinx. I've got some goggles, of course, but they give me only tunnel vision and make me look like something from outer space. I was not sure that if I'd misplaced the glasses and then dropped the lenses I could put my hand on either so I let Betty have a key. I could feel my way to the telephone, dial by touch, and she would have come running. That was the arrangement. They're bloody awful things to find once you've dropped one are contact lenses even with normal sight. I could have asked the Trivetts on the other side of me, I suppose. They're nearer than you are, but they're quite an old couple. Didn't want to bother 'em. So there you are, Leonard. If you get a phone call early one morning it'll be me in distress. Daren't move a foot in case I step on a lens I've dropped." Miss Tatchell roared with laughter, and Beckworth found himself grinning in sympathy. She had an infectious sort of laugh.

"Don't worry," she went on having opened the back door and bawled for the dog, "it hasn't happened yet and I don't suppose it ever will now, but when I first had the lenses, soon after the op, there was a grave danger of it, I can tell you. Still, stick to the key, if you don't mind. If I'm ever away you can keep an eye on the place for me. It's a reciprocal arrangement, come to that, because I've got one to the bungalow. Mrs. Nash has been using it. So long, Len. Don't forget to look in for that drink."

When she had gone Beckworth scratched his head and said "Cripes!" out loud. Overpowering was what most people would have described her as being, he thought, but he liked her in spite of it. He'd not much use for women as a rule. Most of those whom he had come into contact with had not bothered to hide their disapproval or contempt for his overall shabbiness and his obvious liking for strong ale. He had never met one before who had actually asked him to call upon her for a drink. If Cynthia had lived, he reflected, she would have been a lot like Miss Tatchell, same eyes and same figure. But only to look at. She wouldn't have been calling a spade a spade as the laughing Miss Tatchell did. People were undoubtedly more trusting in the country. That business of the keys. She must have two keys to the bungalow because the solicitors had said that they'd given her one. She must have passed it on to the cleaning lady. Beckworth's training as a policeman wouldn't let him accept easily this carefree passing of keys to property amongst neighbours. The country was undoubtedly different.

He learnt quite a bit about Miss

Tatchell from gossiping in the village pub. She was forty-eight years old, the last of the Tatchells, and she was generally reckoned to have been pretty free with her favours in the past, possibly the reason she had never married. She lived alone in the old Edwardian house which had been her parents' home. There were some lurid stories about her, which Beckworth rather resented hearing. He did his best to pin somebody down and make them say that the details were authentic but never succeeded. In his opinion she was one hell of a woman whom he liked.

Gradually he fitted himself into his new life. He couldn't find himself a job; not one that would appeal to him but now that he was a man of property it was not urgent. He had enough. He worked hard in the garden and there was no doubt that the exercise did him good. He saw a lot of Tatch, as the village called her, and was a frequent visitor to Orchard House. She was often in the pub and called upon him at the bungalow. His old life in North London seemed as remote as if it had been lived on another planet and there were times when he found it difficult to recollect that he had been a cop in contact with the sordid, the vicious, and the cruel that went hand-in-hand with villainy. Life in the country was so gentle in comparison.

Then one morning in early June he received a telephone call from Miss Tatchell that, although he didn't know it, was to bring it all back in no uncertain way. He was in the garden inspecting the first roses. The dew was still on them and the air was redolent with the smell of them. He hurried indoors to answer the call.

"Leonard," she started off without preamble, "it's happened. Remember I told you that I had an old uncle in the States who'd made me his heir, or heiress, I suppose it should be?"

"Chicken farmer, wasn't he?"

"And how! He's left me a packet, Len. I'm bloody dazed . . . but, listen. He's only just snuffed it but the news is out and the publicity is going to be enormous.

I'm dodging it, I hope. Larkin my solicitor is in a bit of a panic. He's tried to keep it quiet but it's started in the States and it will be in today's evening papers. The television crews have already rung up and I've told 'em to get stuffed. I'm going away for a bit, Len, right now and that's why I'm ringing you . . . if you'll keep an eye on the place till I get back?"

"Of course. Where are you going?"

"Not far. Brighton or Eastbourne maybe. Yeah, Eastbourne, I think. I know an old hotel there where they'll take Butch. It's antediluvian but I shan't be bothered at all."

"Want me to drive you?"

He knew that she had her own small car which she used for pottering round the district but was nervous of the main roads because of her sight.

"Nice of you to ask, Len, but I'll go by rail. I've ordered a taxi from Chichester. See you in about a couple of weeks, eh? It'll be a seven-day wonder and then forgotten."

"Well, I'm glad about the inheritance for your sake," he said awkwardly.

"Bit embarrassing really. Larkin says I won't get my hands on it for some time. See you, Len. 'Bye!"

She came in for a good deal of discussion in the local at lunch time. Passing her house on his way Beckworth noticed a number of cars parked along the road and groups of pressmen gathered round the front door. How much had she inherited, for God's sake? She'd dodged them all evidently.

It was not until the next morning that he heard any details. He made a point of collecting his daily paper rather than have it delivered because the walk into the village and back ensured him some exercise. The newsagent knew all about the inheritance.

"See our Miss Tatchell is in the news," he commented. "Come into a fortune. Five million dollars from some old uncle in the States. How d'you like that?"

He showed Beckworth some headlines. His own paper which was notoriously low in journalistic worth but renowned for its photographs gave it a line or two headed "Tasmin's Jackpot." Others more conservative said: "British Woman inherits American Fortune," and another cried: "Lone Spinster's Windfall."

The newsagent gave him the gist of it and knew all about her.

"He was a Beamish, her mother's brother," he told Beckworth. "They all came from around these parts originally. She'd be the last of 'em, I reckon. Appears the old chap had a chicken farm in Texas, and they found oil under it. Can't be bad, can it?

"Good for Tatch anyway. She's pushed off to dodge the publicity . . . went yesterday. I guess she's made it . . . you can't see any photographs of her in this lot." He gestured at the newspapers laid out along the counter.

The sergeant thought little more about it except for the inevitable gossiping in the local. It was a change in the weather that brought Miss Tatchell to mind again. The early June sunshine gave way to wind and rain almost continually for four days. The rain was heavy at times, and Beckworth decided to take a look at Orchard House sooner than he would have done had the weather stayed fine. It was an old place. There might be leaks or she might have left a window open somewhere in the excited state of mind she'd been in before she had left.

But he found nothing amiss. It was a comfortable Edwardian house with high ceilings and plenty of space in all of its rooms. Beckworth could not think why she kept up such a big place living alone as she did. It was a bit too gloomy for his liking because of the surrounding trees, at any rate in the front downstairs rooms. Upstairs the rooms were lighter especially at the back where they looked over a wide and long garden mostly lawn. Although retired Beckworth glanced at everything with a policeman's inquisitive mind, which was why when gazing out at the back lawn he spotted an irregularity in the surface of a flower bed. The room he was in had been a nursery at one time.

Indeed it still contained an old fashioned rocking horse which challenged Beckworth's presence with a glassy eye. He tried to imagine Miss Tatchell as a girl astride its spotted grey flanks, and failed utterly. He decided that something had been buried recently in the flower bed. The recent rain had made it obvious. He went downstairs and out of the back door to the big circular bed roughly in its middle.

It was an area three feet by two that had been disturbed, he saw. The petunias in the bed which had obviously been dug out and hastily replaced had still not recovered. They looked upset, somehow. He wondered what it was beneath them. The house had contained its usual silver and bric-a-brac as far as he could recall. No treasure under there. She wouldn't have been so silly and she wouldn't have had the time, he thought.

He found a spade in the garden shed. Its blade went in easily through the damp mould. He expected it to strike a solid object before it had gone far but though it sort of clogged on an obstruction it was not solid. He pushed the soil around gently and saw what looked like white curly hair. Two minutes later he had unearthed the animal's battered head. The red collar was still round its narrow neck and the red lead had been wrapped round its body. No doubt about it, the remains of Miss Tatchell's poodle Butch.

2

THE discovery startled Beckworth for a moment. He was too old a hand, and had been present at far grislier finds for it to do more than that. He squatted above it, peering over his enormous stomach. The poor beast had been killed by a blow on its head from an axe or an iron bar perhaps. Its sharp little teeth were bared in a final snarl. He poked around the grave for a bit in case the weapon used had been buried alongside the small victim, but he found nothing. Finally he took up the spade and filled in the pathetic sight, taking care with the petunias.

One thing was certain, he decided. It was not Tatch who had killed her pet. He could imagine her anger at the discovery and the way she would go for the person responsible when found. He could almost see the flailing blows she would aim at the killer's head with her handbag or anything else she could grab. So who had killed the dog, and what was perhaps even more significant, why? She had told him that she would be going to Eastbourne where she knew an hotel to take both her and the dog. Had she for some reason, hard to see, left Butch behind? At the last moment she might have taken the animal to some kennels from which it had escaped and come home. Finding her gone it might have set up a yowling, which had finally got on somebody's nerves to such an extent that the brutal bastard had killed the dog in a rage. Farfetched? Maybe, but strange things happened in isolated communities. However, nobody lived close enough to Orchard House to hear a lonely dog's howling. It was odd coming on top of the news of Tatch's inheritance.

Beckworth was too much of a cop to leave it at that. While he pondered on the event he looked around for a possible weapon, which he thought would more than likely have been discarded immediately it had been used. He searched the garden and looked in the greenhouse. But it was the potting shed that yielded results. Under the bench, right at the back out of sight, was an old chopper. Some white hairs and a trace of blood were along its blunt edge. Beckworth handled it carefully more through force of habit than any thought it might be necessary to test it for fingerprints. He found some brown paper in the shed and wrapped the chopper using a piece of bass to tie it which was all he could find in the way of string.

He was walking down the short drive having locked up the house thinking of his morning glass when a yellow MGB even shabbier than his old Cortina pulled up outside the gate with a squeal of tired brakes. A man about thirty casually dressed in a light blue crew-necked jersey and slacks of a light check pattern pushed out long legs, and stood up brushing back his lank fair hair. He had a long nose, which didn't suit his long hair, and a wispy moustache growing from a wide upper lip. His brown eyes were sharp and as alert as a bird's.

"Hi, man!" he called to Beckworth. "Who's at home? Miss Tatchell back?"

The sergeant's first thought was to tell him to get lost which he would undoubtedly have retorted had he still been on a duty but he realized quite suddenly that he was no longer a person with any sort of authority.

"She's still away," he grunted. "Who are you? A pressman?"

"That's right. West Sussex Globe. Name's Garvey. But you've been in the house, man. I've a look-out down the road with binoculars. He saw you go in and phoned me."

Beckworth grinned. You had to hand it to these news hounds, he thought. They stuck to the chance of a story like glue to a blanket. This one had obviously slipped a pound or two to a neighbour within viewing distance to let him know as soon as Miss Tatchell was back.

"You're out of luck, mister," he told

him and would have gone on, but the younger man stopped him by exclaiming:

"Hang about! I know you, man. I've seen you before. Saw you giving evidence in the Crown Court eight . . . nine months ago against a gang of bullion thieves. You're a cop!"

"Not any more. I'm retired now." Beckworth shook his head. "I'm a neighbour of Miss Tatchell's who asked me to keep an eye on the house while she's away. Now, don't ask me where she is because I don't know and I wouldn't tell you if I did."

Garvey had immediately seen such possibilities in the idea of a policeman calling at Orchard House that his face crumpled in dismay when he learnt the truth. Beckworth felt almost sorry for him. He also felt slightly flattered that he should have been recognized from an earlier visit to Chichester. This Garvey was a bright boy really on the ball. Having to admit that he was now retired had brought home to Beckworth again that he was indeed nothing but a neighbour as powerless as the next man. But he had a minor mystery on his mind. It scratched away there worrying him. The killing of the poodle was a deed that would be so utterly repugnant to its owner that he could not help worrying about Tatch herself. Had anything happened to her? He intended to find out and not knowing where she was didn't help. Could he enlist the aid of this young newspaper chap?

"Tell you what," he said on impulse. "I could have a story for you. I can't promise anything but there might be one in the offing. I'm on my way to the local for the morning jar. Care to join me?"

The hint of a story drew Garvey like a salmon to a tasty lure. He walked round his battered car and opened its passenger door.

"Hop in, man," he invited.

The MGB covered the short distance to the pub in a matter of seconds. Beckworth thought it was like sitting in a rather fast bucket.

When he had exchanged greetings with

the regulars present he led Garvey to his favourite corner as soon as he had bought two pints of best bitter.

"Now get this straight, son," he declared after they had pledged each other, "what I have to tell you is *not* for publication. Not yet. Not till I say so. I want your solemn oath on that or . . . nothing doing."

"Sure, man. You've got it. How's about giving me your name? You've had mine."

"Beckworth. Detective Sergeant retired. No. 8 Regional Crime Squad. Where do you hail from? You talk like a Spade. This 'man' business, I mean."

"South Africa, Mr. Beckworth. Been over here a year and a half. Aim to get to Fleet Street, but you have to start in the provinces. But Chichester, a cathedral city . . . strictly quietsville."

"What do your friends call you?"

"Tom."

"Right, Tom. I'm Len. Here's what's worrying me, OK, I've been in Miss Tatchell's house. She left me a key. But in the garden . . ." He related how he had found the dead poodle. "It worries me," he went on. "She's not the sort of woman to kill a pet or stand by and let somebody else do it. In fact she's more like one of those crazy dames who leaves a bloody animal a couple of thousand quid in her will. So what's behind it?"

Garvey finished his beer. He had a prominent Adam's apple that bobbed up and down as he drank.

"Sounds queer enough," he admitted. "But a pet dog, man. What makes you so concerned?"

"For Pete's sake!" Beckworth exclaimed. "The woman has just inherited five million dollars. That could make her a target for all the bloody chisellers in the country. God knows, you news guys print enough about it. Beats me why you have to do it."

"It's what the great English Public likes to read, Len. Next best thing to coming into a packet yourself is to read about some other guy who has. What you'd call a vicarious thrill, I guess. You think

30

someone is aiming to do the old dame out of her inheritance then?"

"I don't know, Tom. But I've been a cop for thirty years, and I just don't like finding my neighbour's dog, dead and buried in her garden, when she's supposed to have taken it with her. And Miss Tatchell ain't all that old. Forty-eight and looks a lot younger."

Garvey gathered their two empty tankards, took them to the bar, had them refilled, and brought them back to their table.

"Are you sweet on her then?" he asked.

Beckworth snorted half scornfully and half in indignation.

"Be your age, son. Who'd want an old beer swiller like me? No. She's a good sort. I wouldn't want anything to happen to her."

"How can it, man? I mean . . . this fortune she's inherited. It'll be handled by lawyers through banks. What will you do? You say you don't know where she is?"

"She told me that she was going either

to Brighton or Eastbourne. She went by rail. Her car's still in her garage. She favoured Eastbourne, said there was an old hotel there she knew would let her have the dog. That's what baffles me. She phoned me the same morning. Five days ago. I'm no expert but by the look of the animal's corpse it could've been killed on the same day."

Garvey sat with both hands round his tankard while he thought about matters.

"Real odd, Len. Seems to me you'll have to find the lady. There might be an explanation. Do you know her solicitors?"

"I know his name is . . . Larkin, I think she said."

Garvey took a gulp at his beer.

"Larkin, Brown and Larkin," he told Beckworth. "They occupy some old premises in North Pallant in the city. Brown's dead, so it's Larkin and Son now. Larkin senior is in semi-retirement, which leaves Charles Larkin, the son, as the principal working partner. And, man, you can have that Zulu."

Beckworth raised his eyebrows.

"How come you know so much about 'em?" he asked.

"I did the obit on Octavius Brown, prominent citizen of Chichester. I interviewed Charlie Larkin. Strictly Snotsville is Charlie. There was some talk of them taking in another partner. Maybe they have. I wish him luck with Charlie. Anything I can do to help, Len? The old *Globe* ain't exactly without resources when it comes to finding folk provided it has a starting point, so to speak."

"Thanks. How about making enquiries in Brighton? I reckon I can manage Eastbourne."

"Can do. If she's in an hotel under her own name it won't be difficult because . . . trade secret . . . we keep contacts in most of the prominent hotels in Sussex."

"Wait till I've seen Larkin. I'll give you a bell afterwards."

They would have left it at that, but when Beckworth finished his beer and showed signs of departure Garvey said:

"I'll have a bite of lunch here, man.

They keep a pretty good cold collation by the look of the counter."

Beckworth had felt a liking for the younger man and although he had lived alone for years he had always eaten with others for company. He was still not used to lonely meals by himself.

"Come home with me," he offered. "I'm on my own. Cold turkey with a slice of York ham. How does that grab you? I can have a lift in your yellow bucket."

Garvey accepted. He was somewhat taken with this retired cop, whom he considered an unusual character and well worth cultivating. They exchanged telephone numbers and got moving.

After lunch when Garvey had gone the sergeant decided that he would call upon Larkin, Brown and Larkin. There was a chance that they knew Miss Tatchell's whereabouts though it was a much fainter one that they would be prepared to let him know where she was, but it was worth trying.

Beckworth's opinion of solicitors in general was a poor one gained from his dealings with them over the years. He thought that far too many of them were muddlers sheltered by the Law Society and its closed shop from the consequences of their own incompetence. Most of those he had come into contact with, however, had been representing some pretty ripe villains and had not themselves been exactly jewels of their profession.

He didn't expect to find Larkin, Brown and Larkin to be much different from countless other small firms. Certainly their premises, a dingy reception desk at the top of a flight of brown linoleum covered stairs and a small general office behind the counter containing the usual clutter of filing cabinets, a couple of desks, typewriters and piles of pink be-ribboned documents on shelves, did nothing to dispel the idea.

The staff were not all that numerous; two clerks and two typists were all he could see until he punched the old-fashioned brass bell on the counter top, then a tousle-haired youth as lean as a bean pole made his way to the counter.

Beckworth told him he would like to see Mr. Charles Larkin and gave him his name and rank without telling him he was retired. The boy with absolutely no change of expression said: "Hang about," and went off to disappear within a glass enclosed cubicle at the back of the office. Beckworth could see a man at a desk within to whom the boy spoke. The individual got up and came towards the counter. The sergeant saw that he was a huge fellow. He stated his business again.

"Oh, dear," the giant said in such a pansy-like voice that Beckworth gaped at him unashamedly, "I don't think Mr. Larkin will want to see you without an appointment, sir. I'm sure he won't. Is there anything I can do? I'm Mr. Deacon, his managing clerk."

Beckworth recovering from the voice was further prejudiced against Mr. Deacon by the man's use of a mister in front of his own name. Apart from his size which made him a freak, Deacon appeared to be a bundle of contrasts. He had a sallow complexion, dark hair clipped short on his skull, and black eyes set above a hooky sort of nose. The eyes were as hard as coal and full of suspicion, at complete variance with his humble attitude and namby-pamby voice as he stood stooping, hands the size of dinner plates clasped in front of him. What the hell was the man so wary of? Was it because he thought the visitor to be a policeman on duty?

The sergeant realized that he could not insist upon seeing Charles Larkin much as he would have liked to have done. He said that he wanted to learn Miss Tatchell's whereabouts in order to inform her of the death of her pet. He related how he had come upon the poodle's body.

"Oh, I say! What a dreadful thing!" Deacon exclaimed. Beckworth felt sure the man must be a poof. "Mr. Larkin will want to know about this. Will you wait a moment, sir? You're not on duty now, I suppose?"

"Retired," Beckworth grunted. "Miss Tatchell and I are neighbours."

Deacon disappeared into the back

regions. Presently he returned to take Beckworth on a circuitous route round the general office and into a private room.

"This is Detective Sergeant Beckworth retired, Mr. Larkin, sir," Deacon announced him.

The solicitor was seated at a large desk cluttered with files and papers which seemed to be a feature of every lawyer's desk Beckworth had ever seen. Larkin was in his forties. He had a squarish sort of head with sparse red hair, bulbous blue eyes noticeably veined and bloodshot, and a sneering mouth. His upper lip looked to be permanently lifted as if at one time it had been damaged and somehow shortened. He had a rasping sort of voice distinctly hostile which didn't endear him to Beckworth any more than his appearance.

"My clerk tells me you're seeking Miss Tatchell's present address. Is that so?" he began without preamble or without offering Beckworth a chair.

"That's right."

"Why?"

"Didn't he tell you that? I found her pet dog dead and buried in her garden, and I thought she should be told about it."

"You know, I suppose, that she has come into a good deal of money?"

"She rang me the morning she went away to tell me as much. She went off to dodge the publicity."

Larkin reached for a box of cigarettes, took one out and put a light to it. He failed to offer one to his visitor, who wouldn't have taken one if he had but who added the failure to his rapidly mounting dislike of the red-headed solicitor.

"I can't help you I'm afraid. As far as I know she was going to take the damned dog with her. We warned her of the coming publicity. We would have kept it entirely confidential, of course, but the Americans let the cat out of the bag. What exactly is your interest in Miss Tatchell?" Larkin blew smoke across the desk.

39

"A neighbourly one."

"And you're a Detective Sergeant, retired? From the local force?"

"Metropolitan."

"And now she's come into a fortune you see some pickings for yourself, I suppose?" Larkin sneered.

Beckworth controlled himself with an effort. He recalled how Garvey had told him of his own dislike of Larkin. "You can have that Zulu," he'd said. The sergeant wondered what Garvey had against the Zulus. He decided that he didn't want any part of Charles Larkin or his creeping hulk of a managing clerk like something out of a horror film. Deacon's supplicant attitude in the presence of his employer was even more preposterous than the one he had displayed outside.

"There's only one thing I want from Miss Tatchell, Larkin," Beckworth said deliberately avoiding the courtesy of a mister, "and I'll make bloody sure I get it from her."

"And what's that?"

40

"To hear that she's changed her solicitor. Good day to you."

Beckworth walked out.

41

3

THE sergeant had not expected much from his visit to Miss Tatchell's solicitors and was in no way disappointed, merely hot under the collar at the reception he'd had from Charles Larkin.

Beckworth ambled along to the Post Office and a telephone where he was able to contact Tom Garvey, who said that he would set enquiries going in Brighton to cover the chance of Miss Tatchell having registered in an hotel there. He suggested that he called upon Beckworth, not that evening but the next, to report progress if any and to have another go at his excellent York ham by way of supper.

"Fair enough," the sergeant agreed. "If I'm not at home you'll find me in the pub."

He then went round the corner to the public library where in the reference section he found a guide book which gave him the names and telephone numbers of every hotel in Eastbourne. If he were to call them all it would add considerable weight to his telephone bill so he made a list of likely ones from the information given bearing in mind that Miss Tatchell had described the one she favoured as being antediluvian. He would check it further against an AA handbook he had at home. It might be a good idea also to take another look inside Orchard House before he started telephoning. There was a faint chance that she had some documentary evidence of where she had stayed before in Eastbourne about the house; an old bill head or an hotel marked in a tourist guide, perhaps, lying around in her desk.

He realized that he was going to considerable trouble on the lady's behalf, and he thought to himself, why not? Apart from the fact that he liked her he was genuinely concerned about the bizarre discovery of her slaughtered pet. It was such an incongruous happening, so utterly alien to the gentle nature of life where they both lived that he could not help wondering if anything had befallen Tatch herself. It might help to know whether or not she had actually taken the dog with her when she had left.

The yellow pages of the telephone directory gave him the names and addresses of taxi and car hire firms in the city. There was one in South Street which he thought must be a favourite for traffic to and from the station and he made this his first call.

This was real old fashioned police work, which he considered no effort at all though it was unusual for him to pull a prize first time as he did on this occasion. The office had a record of a telephone call from Orchard House, Funtingdon on the morning in question to bring a passenger to the railway station.

"'Ang about, guv," the man in the office invited. He apparently dropped his aitches as freely as he did his dandruff. "'Erb 'Arper was the driver. 'E'll be in soon."

In due course a diesel cab rumbled into the yard and the office man pointed a biro at it. "That's 'im, guv."

Beckworth had an old warrant card which he was prepared to flash quite illegally in order to get information if needed, but it was not required. Harper, the driver, was a tall gangling youth and amiable, though the mandarin moustache he affected made him look incredibly sad. He remembered taking Miss Tatchell to the station five days previously.

"Yeah," he said. "A tall dame. She give me a good tip. I remember her. She had a loud voice."

"Did she have a dog with her . . . a white poodle?"

The driver shook his head slowly as if he was not convinced and then came out firmly with:

"No. But I remember now. There was one in the house. Barking its head off, it was. They didn't come out straightaway soon as I got there as a lot of folk do so I switched off, got out of the cab and rang the doorbell. That's when I heard the dog."

"*They* didn't come out?" Beckworth echoed. "You mean she wasn't alone?"

"Well, she come out of the house alone. I took her suitcase, see? While I was making for the cab with it I heard her saying goodbye to somebody."

"D'you see who it was? Man or woman?"

"No, mister. I wasn't paying 'em any attention."

"Thanks a lot, Mr. Harper," Beckworth told him. "You've been a great help. Have a drink on me, eh?"

He handed him a pound note which the driver acknowledged by putting a finger to an eyebrow.

The sergeant was intrigued by what he had learnt. Who had been in the house then when she had left? Had it been her solicitor? From what he could recall of the telephone conversation with Miss Tatchell early that morning Beckworth had received the impression that Larkin had been with her at the time. But if he had he would have known that she'd not taken the dog. Perhaps he had known, the sergeant thought, but out of sheer bloodymindedness had said or suggested the opposite. Beckworth, whose mind still rankled with the treatment he had been given by Larkin, was quite prepared to believe the solicitor had killed the dog himself. Perhaps at the last minute Tatch had decided to put the dog into kennels and asked Larkin to do it or to see it was done. Then, maybe enraged by the animal's continued barking the solicitor, just the type to kick a dog in Beckworth's estimation, had booted it one hurting it badly enough to warrant putting the poor beast out of its misery. Jesus! If that happened Tatch, when she learnt the truth, would need no encouragement at all to change her solicitor. But as far as he could recall, and he was not by any means expert, the only injury he had seen on the dog's carcass had been its crushed head. So what the hell *had* happened?

He was still of the opinion that Miss Tatchell should be told what had happened and at the back of his policeman's mind was the nagging suspicion that all might not be well with her.

When he had driven home and had made himself a cup of tea (the mid-afternoon cuppa was the only one of the day) he thought that he would go along to Orchard House and take another look round as he had promised himself before he started his telephoning which at any rate he would not attempt till after six p.m. when the calls would be cheaper.

As he was about to open the gate to the drive of Miss Tatchell's house he spotted a figure stumping along with a stick towards him from the direction of the village. He thought it might be Colonel Trivett whom he had never met but had seen going into his house up the road before then. The figure raised the walking stick on high as if wanting a word with him and Beckworth waited for the old gentleman to reach him.

Colonel Trivett conformed to type in that he had a white cavalry moustache, a red hooky nose and a fierce blue eye. He was sparse of figure and neatly turned out in twill fawn trousers and a hacking jacket of excellent cut. He was wearing a cap made of the same tweed, the brim of which had been bent to lend it a rakish air.

"My name's Trivett," he introduced himself. "You must be Mrs. Timpson's brother . . ."

"Beckworth. Leonard Beckworth."

"How d'yer do? I knew your sister slightly . . . nodding terms, y'know. Miss Tatchell left you her key, did she? At least she told my wife she had. Come to something when a poor woman has to run away from home to dodge publicity just because she's come into a bit of money, eh?"

"That's how it is, sir."

Beckworth wondered how much he could confide in the colonel, who, after all, was a closer neighbour to Miss Tatchell than he was and probably had known her for a number of years.

"I looked over the house earlier," he

went on. "Everything is in order, but I'm a retired copper, sir, and maybe I see trouble where it doesn't exist, but . . ." he told the colonel of his discovery of the dog's carcass under the flower bed.

"Good grief!" the old man exclaimed. "Her own dog . . . killed, you say? She'll go raving mad as soon as she learns about it. Have you told her yet?"

"I don't know where she is, but I thought she should know. As a matter of fact I was about to take another look in the house to see if I could find some clue to where she's staying. Eastbourne or Brighton I think. How well do you know her, sir? She may be staying in an old hotel at Eastbourne she's used before. Perhaps she told you its name some time."

"Agnes, my wife, might know it. She certainly has never told me," the colonel mused, and went on: "We've known Tatch for years of course being neighbours but let's face it, she ain't exactly our cup of tea or we hers. Generation gap for a start. Damn it, I'm nearly eighty and my wife's not far off it. We're a crotchety old couple, I daresay, and you know Miss Tatchell. A live wire, eh? Swears like a marine and was supposed to have been pretty free with her favours when she was younger. Well, why not? Dashed handsome woman, and still is, come to that." The colonel's smile transfixed his lean old face and his eyes twinkled. "So we can't claim real friendship but I suppose you could say that our relationship has always been cordial, eh? Though it had a bit of a setback the morning the lady departed."

"How was that, sir?" Beckworth asked.

"Nothing really, but you know what women are. Tatch rang us first thing on the Wednesday morning . . ."

"She rang me too. Gave me the news of the inheritance and that she was going away to dodge the publicity."

"Exactly. Well, I took the call . . . wished her well, that sort of thing." The colonel tweaked his moustache. "Quite forgot that Agnes might want a word with her. Anyway my wife decided to pop down the road and to have a quick word with Tatch. Wanted to hear all about the inheritance, I daresay, though she made the excuse that if Tatch was leaving home somebody ought to have a key to Orchard House to look in now and again especially if it was about to be besieged by the Press. We didn't know then that you had a key."

The colonel paused as if inviting comment but Beckworth only nodded and the old gentleman went on:

"Nobody outside the house when she got here." He pointed at the house with his stick. "One car in the drive. Larkin, her solicitor, had come in that and it was he who opened the front door to her ring and let her inside . . . reluctantly, Agnes thought."

"Do you know Larkin, the solicitor, sir?"

"Used the firm a bit. Yes, they're my solicitors you might say though I haven't been near 'em since I made me will twenty years ago." Colonel Trivett snorted. "It was the youngster who let in

Agnes, not old George. He's in semi-retirement now they say. Ha! Never been in any other state in my opinion. Golfing fanatic, y'know. Always thought more of keeping an appointment on the first tee at Goodwood than he did with a client. But I was telling you what happened when Agnes called."

"Sorry. I side-tracked you."

"Well, Larkin let Agnes in. Larkin's clerk was there as well, big hulking fellow . . . can't remember his name . . ."

"Deacon."

"That's it. Both he and his wife were there. Larkin said something about his car being out of action so the two had run him into Funtingdon first thing. He'd thought it essential that Miss Tatchell be warned in time to dodge the publicity. He'd thought a personal visit would impress it upon her that life would be unbearable for two or three days the Press were so persistent, unless she went away."

"That's true enough, sir, God knows.

Newspaper reporters can be an absolute bloody nuisance."

"Yes. From what I know of Miss Tatchell though she would have rather enjoyed sending 'em packing with fleas in their ears. However, Larkin persuaded her to go. He'd have had some experience of 'em himself. Silly young so-and-so got himself involved with a well-known actress who was playing the Festival Theatre a couple of years ago. His wife divorced him. Bloody idiot hadn't the sense to keep his fancy women quiet. Where was I?"

"Your wife had just been let into the house," Beckworth grinned.

"Ah, yes. Well, that's about all there was to it. Larkin said that Tatch was upstairs packing but he'd go and tell her Agnes had called. So she waited there with this great hulk of a feller, Deacon, standing over her with his hands clasped in front of him, and his wife standing alongside not saying a word, and the damned dog barking its head off somewhere. Got on her nerves, a bit, she said.

She reckoned this Deacon feller to be nothing but a bloody great nancy boy. Anyway, Larkin came down with a message from Tatch. She was in the middle of packing, would Agnes excuse her, it was very kind of her to call but Mr. Beckworth down the road had a key to the house and would keep an eye on it, and Tatch would write to her as soon as she got a chance."

The colonel did his moustache twitching act.

"That was that. Agnes was a bit huffed, I don't mind telling you, but there it is . . . you can never tell how the individual will react when he or she suddenly becomes wealthy overnight. If Tatch were my age she'd know that the simple pleasures of life are the best. Given good health, a full belly, a roof over your head and a spot of brandy now and again what the hell else do you need, eh?"

"You've got a point there, sir," Beckworth acknowledged. "Do you know anything about dogs?"

"Quite a bit. Used to breed Airedale

terriers. Vanishing now. What's that got to do with it?"

"I'd like you to look at the corpse of Tatch's poodle if you would. It's in the garden. What I want to find out is whether it was killed deliberately out of hand, so to speak, or because it had suffered some other injury and was put out of its misery. I'm not expert enough."

"Take it to a vet. There's not one in the village, though."

"I don't want too many people to know of this," Beckworth hedged. "I don't mind telling you, sir, that it's got me worried. It's . . . it's so completely . . . I don't know how to describe it . . . inconsistent? I can't help feeling that there might be some bigger reason, other than hitting a dog on the head, behind it."

The colonel thought about this tapping the ferrule of his stick on the gravel of Miss Tatchell's drive-in.

"Well, you're a policeman . . ." he began.

"I'm a Detective Sergeant retired with no authority whatsoever, sir, but I'm also the lady's neighbour, same as you. Will you take a look at the dog? I've established that it must have been killed after Tatch left the house." He told the colonel how he had traced the taxi driver who'd taken her to the station.

The old man nodded.

"Have you spoken to Larkin?"

"He says that as far as he knows she proposed taking the animal with her. But I think he was lying. The cab driver says she said goodbye to somebody . . . he didn't see who . . . in the house where the dog was barking."

"And you think that was Larkin?"

"Don't know who else it could have been."

"But why should he lie about it?"

"I don't think it was deliberate, sir. Just a quickie to get rid of me . . . he probably said it without thinking."

"Well, all right. Let's have a look at the animal then."

They went up the drive and round the house to the back garden. Beckworth fetched a spade from the garden shed and very quickly dug up the dog's corpse again.

The colonel stabbed his walking stick into the garden bed out of the way, took out a pair of steel rimmed spectacles, hooked these on and stooped to examine the grisly object. He ran bony fingers down its legs and along the ribs. He inspected the jaws, forcing the mouth open to see the tongue.

"I doubt if it was poisoned," he gave his opinion, "and certainly none of its bones were broken, but as you said of yourself, I'm no expert. I'd say that it was a perfectly healthy animal killed by a blow on the head."

Beckworth interred the corpse once again. Before the colonel took his leave the sergeant hinted that it would be as well to keep the incident as quiet as possible at least till he had seen Miss Tatchell and learnt her reaction to it. He walked down the drive with the old gentleman and watched him stumping away up the road bringing his stick down on the tarmac as if he hated the stuff.

When he had gone Beckworth let himself into the house and made for what he knew Tatch called her workroom where she had a small desk, a sewing machine and shelves full of books. The desk was locked but that didn't worry him much. It was a simple lock he could have opened with a hairpin but in fact, trying the smaller keys on his own bunch, he found one that turned with a bit of pressure, and unlocked the desk.

He felt something of a heel prying into the pigeon holes. They contained what he wanted, a stack of receipted bills but there was nothing amongst them from an hotel. He found her cheque book. She banked with Carrs branch in East Street, Chichester. He thought it odd that she had not taken it with her, but he was not looking for that sort of thing. He found two sets of contact lenses in little blue cases put away in a pigeon hole, and again he thought it odd that she'd not taken a set with her if they were her spares.

The desk yielded him no information at all concerning a likely hotel and he relocked it. He had better luck on the bookshelves. She had a number of old AA handbooks. He whipped through these looking under Eastbourne and in the one for 1976 he found a pencil mark against the Tarnwood Hotel. He made a note of its number.

He thought that he ought to examine the rest of the house whilst he was there; a little more closely perhaps than he had first time because he could not help feeling that all might not be well with the owner after the discovery of her dead pet. Perhaps he was imagining things. Maybe after a long lay-off from any sort of police work he was enjoying the mystery to such an extent he was ignoring common sense. But he found nothing unusual, only a set of glasses with enormously thick lenses tucked away in their leatherbound case in a bedroom drawer. He thought she would have taken them with her. She must have several spares.

He didn't wait till six o'clock before ringing the Tarnwood Hotel but dialled the number as soon as he was back in the bungalow.

"Yes," a female voice, so refined it sounded as if it were hurting its owner to use it, answered his query, "we have a Miss Tesmin Tetchell staying here but she has left specific instructions that we are not to accept any telephone calls. So sorry."

"She'll take one from me," Beckworth said. "Push it, lady. My name's Beckworth."

"Heng on, please."

The line went dead but presently it came spluttering back.

"So sorry. She is not in the hotel."

"Well, give her a message, please. I'll be calling upon her tomorrow morning at eleven o'clock. Or she can ring me if she's back before seven this evening."

He was not going to delay the start of the night's socializing any longer for her. In a way he hoped she wouldn't ring because what he had to tell her might be better told her in person. Not so much of a shock.

She failed to telephone, however, either that evening or the next morning. It was a fine one and Beckworth enjoyed the drive to Eastbourne though the traffic on the coastal road was nearing congestion.

The Tarnwood Hotel was on high ground at the back of the town, an old Victorian structure all gables and corners standing in its own grounds. The receptionist was the lady with the ultra-refined voice, which Beckworth recognized. She was an arid-looking blonde with bony shoulders.

"So sorry," she bleated in answer to his request. "Miss Tetchell left us this morning without giving us a forwarding address."

4

BECKWORTH was not only surprised but hurt and angry to hear that Miss Tatchell had gone. What the hell was she playing at? Had she received his telephone message of the previous evening?

It was the receptionist's turn to feel upset when he suggested that she had failed to pass on the message. She grew positively frigid but when the sergeant gave her a grudging apology she condescended to fetch the hall porter who had seen Miss Tatchell off the premises and carried her suitcase.

He proved to be an old man, bald as an egg, and wearing steel-rimmed glasses with pebble lenses as solid as the thick end of bottles. Beckworth's heart sank when he saw him. He knew instinctively that the old chap would not be of any use. Yes, she'd gone in a car. No, he didn't know if it had been a taxi. She'd not asked him to get her one. Colour of the car? Gawd knows, mister. It had been a dark one. No, he'd not heard her give the driver any instructions.

It had gone pretty well as Beckworth had imagined. The old chap had brought out her suitcase, passed it on to the driver, then held out his hand for the tip, and God bless you lady.

The sergeant thought she might have returned home but Orchard House was empty when he got back, nor was there anybody occupying it when he passed later that evening on his way to the local. He had waited some time expecting Garvey to show up at the bungalow as promised but there had been no sign of him, nor did he turn up at the pub during the evening's session, which lasted Beckworth till closing time. He was feeling fed up. Tatch had disappointed him. He recalled the colonel's words of how you can never tell what effect the descent of wealth might have on the individual. He had not really wanted to subscribe to that with its suggestion of a sudden change in character. Not with Miss Tatchell, whom he thought nothing would have changed from the breezy outspoken good-hearted woman he had grown to like. But old Trivett was ancient enough to have known it happen a few times, perhaps, and he might have been right.

Beckworth walked home. No lights burning in Orchard House. Apart from his disappointment over Tatch having ignored his phone call there was his irritation at not being able to solve the mystery set up by the killing of her dog. Whatever the effect of her inheritance it certainly would not have made her in any way condone the crude and brutal killing of a pet poodle. So what had been behind that?

He was still thinking about it as he approached the bungalow. The night was fine with a half-moon glaring and paling the myriad of stars dusting the midnight blue of the heavens. Haymaking was in progress not far distant and the settling dew was bringing the sweet scent of cut grass over the fields.

Beckworth noticed an old car drawn up on the verges of the road about seventy yards from the bungalow. It had not been there when he had gone out and, policeman-like, he wondered about it. When he drew level he saw that it was empty and that it was a Ford Zephyr many years old. In fact he was able to see that it had what he termed mentally an A registration. He didn't bother to work out what year that had been. The moonlight revealed that the car was battered beyond belief. It disguised the colouring, however. Beckworth thought it might be red. He hoped that it had not been abandoned because it would be an eyesore and a nuisance to get rid of if it had. He thought no more about it and turned in at his gate.

He was halfway along the short drive to his front door when the attack came. They had concealed themselves behind the front hedge till he was through the gateway with the idea of coming at him

66

from behind. But they had to move quickly and their feet slurred on the gravel. Beckworth heard them; two men, hooded in Mickey Mouse masks and carrying pick helves or the like. He saw their black shapes silhouetted against the moonlit sky and knew in an instant that his peril was deadly.

He had been taught to defend himself against attack and the more active life he had been leading since he had moved to Funtingdon had made him a fitter man but compared with his attackers he was sluggish. He could not have been otherwise with his customary evening's quota of beer awash in his belly and his reactions dulled by alcohol. He stepped into the path of the nearer of the two and kneed him viciously in the groin before the hefted pick handle could find his head. The man screeched like a pig in torment. His companion only a second behind him had an easier task. Beckworth was slow to recover from his effort and tried to get a grasp on the pick helve of the man he had kneed. He could smell the desperation in his attackers. They gave off an acrid sort of stink like the smell of a farmyard. The second man's club found the side of his head, dazing him. He saw a myriad of pinpoint lights dancing in front of him, but he had the first man's club and fought back furiously. For a short time he held his own driving his attacker towards the gate. But the first man, who had dropped to the ground, recovered sufficiently to grab at Beckworth's ankle and pull him back. A club found the sergeant's head for the second time and the world swayed around him. The next blow felled him. He automatically adopted a foetal curl to protect his vital parts but he was clubbed again and again as he lay on the grass of his lawn till oblivion blotted out everything. His attackers hated him now for his resistance. They hit him and booted him. Their shouted epithets as they did so fouled the night air.

The arrival of Garvey saved his life. The reporter driving with his usual abandon brought his MGB with a startling squeal of brakes to a crash halt six inches from Beckworth's gate, its headlights revealing what was happening. It was a second or two before he realized what the masked figures meant or what they were doing, then he was out of the car and vaulting the gate.

The two attackers paused with the advent of the headlamps glaring through the slats of the gate. Garvey's lean figure as it came leaping over the top decided them instantly. One shouted at the other and they fled over the side hedge of the garden into the field and across it to their car. Garvey let them go. He heard the clatter of the starter and the roar from their ancient car as he knelt over Beckworth, observing with a catch of his breath, the blood about the sergeant's head, black in the moonlight. It looked bad. Without more ado Garvey groped in the unconscious man's pockets for his keys. The Zephyr's noisy departure was dying in the distance as he unlocked the front door of the bungalow. The telephone was in the hall.

They would not send an ambulance unless the police were informed as well, something Garvey knew for himself. When he had finished telephoning he went into a bedroom, ripped two blankets off the bed and took them out to the front lawn where he contrived to tuck them round the sergeant's bulky figure without disturbing him too much. The head wounds looked ghastly. Beckworth was breathing with a sort of bubbling noise which Garvey guessed was caused by blood at the back of his throat. It was distressing to hear but there was nothing more he could do except wait for the help that was on its way. He cursed the chance that had made him late arriving for his promised visit. He had been out all day covering a yachting accident in Chichester Creek and had been unable to contact any of the crews concerned till they had eventually come ashore at Bosham harbour. His office had learnt nothing of the whereabouts of Miss Tatchell, but he had not forgotten the promise of supper.

A police patrol car arrived first with a

uniformed sergeant in charge whom Garvey knew. He was acquainted with a number of local policemen, civic dignitaries and local government officials. He made it his business to be so.

Garvey explained how he had come upon the scene and gave them Beckworth's name.

"Don't I know him?" the police sergeant asked, examining Beckworth under the fierce light of a torch.

"More than likely. He's one of you . . . detective sergeant, retired . . . inherited this property from a dead sister and came down here to live. But he was in the city nine or ten months back giving evidence in the Crown Court against a gang of bullion thieves . . ."

"That's right. What's this then? Some of the bastards getting their own back?"

"Hell, man! They're all dead or in gaol. Where's that ambulance?"

It came, after what seemed an age to the anxious Garvey, but was actually with commendable speed. The newspaper man heard it in the distance and had moved his car out of the way before it came to a wailing halt. Within two minutes it was away again with the unconscious Beckworth. Garvey followed.

It took him to St. Richard's Hospital where the head injuries suffered by Beckworth shocked even the hardened medic on duty. But he knew his job and he quickly summoned a neuro-surgeon who worked through the night exerting all his skill and with infinite patience to save not only Beckworth's life but his reason.

Garvey waited till he could see the surgeon. He dozed fitfully in a chair but it was near dawn before he spoke to the man in authority.

"It's bad," the doctor admitted shaking his head. "I won't pretend otherwise, but if he pulls through then he will recover properly. One or two memory lapses, perhaps, but that is all."

Garvey went back to write up his report which was headlined, "Savage attack on retired policeman." He could offer no explanation of it or suggest a motive other than the doubtful one that Beckworth had disturbed the two men as they were about to break into the bungalow, but he himself had seen the pick helves the masked men had been using. Would-be burglars would have been unlikely to have armed themselves with clubs. He speculated on this in the report and nor did he minimise his own part in the action. "Globe reporter's arrival frightens off assailants" was another headline. The *Globe* was published weekly but his report went to the Portsmouth and Brighton evening papers. The national dailies, if they were interested, would pick it up for publication the next day.

It was a week before Beckworth was properly conscious. Before that he was vaguely aware that he was in bed in a darkened room, that his head was swathed in bandages, and that it hurt as if all the hammers that ever were had smashed down on it. He could remember nothing.

Garvey was his first visitor. He arrived in company with a girl friend who was also a fellow employee of the *Globe* where she was a photographer. The reporter had brought Susan Blakeney with him not because he needed photographs but because they were both off duty and it seemed to him to be somehow appropriate to be visiting hospital in company with his girl. It was a disaster. Beckworth could not really get Garvey right in his mind though he recognized him. The presence of a strange female, pretty as she was, still further confused him.

The reporter, who had found a strange liking for the shabby ex-detective in the brief time he had known him, and who had seen his share of the results of violence, was shocked when he saw Beckworth. The room was darkened but he could see the face below the bandaged head bloated with bruises. The injured man's eyes were practically hidden in the swollen flesh. His puffed lips mumbled incomprehensively. But a hand crept out from under the bedclothes and found Garvey's. Beckworth said quite clearly: "Tom."

He could remember nothing of the

actual attack; not at first. The police in the shape of a local CID man Chief Superintendent Rider, whom Beckworth had met on his previous visit to Chichester, called to offer his sympathy in a purely private capacity and to tell him that he had appointed Detective Sergeant Grout to the case. Grout would come in and see Beckworth as soon as the ex-detective sergeant's memory had improved, as the doctors had said it would.

Garvey called regularly. Each time he visited the sick man he brought the conversation round to the days before the attack filling in the gaps in Beckworth's memory, and bit by bit this improved. At first he could not recall Miss Tatchell, not by name. He remembered the morning soon after his arrival in Funtingdon when a handsome woman with a white dog had called at the bungalow opening the front door with a key. He could see her standing in the hall with the dog under her arm.

His memory of the attack came back quite suddenly. The room he was occupying in the hospital was on the ground floor, and its window overlooked a path right outside it. Hospital staff used the paved path and their shadows fell across the glass of his window. One moonlit night when the window had been opened at its top after a burning summer day Beckworth awoke to the clatter of footsteps outside. He opened his eyes as the shadows of two passing medics fell on him and in a flash he was back in his garden with the pick helves raised high to club him and the hoarse breathing of desperate men. He nearly cried out, realized what it was and lay there sweating. But when Detective Sergeant Grout eventually called in to see him he was able to give him an account of what had happened and a description of the two masked figures for what it was worth. Grout was a tall gaunt looking man with a loud trumpeting sort of voice he found difficulty in lowering even in a hospital room. It was obvious that he didn't hold out much hope of finding the two men though Beckworth had remembered and described the old motor car that had brought them to the bungalow.

"Doesn't sound as if burglary was intended," he admitted. "Are you sure some villains from your past ain't caught up with you?"

"Those I've put away wouldn't work off a grudge on an arresting copper," Beckworth said.

Grout's bony fingers plucked off a grape from the bunch brought by Garvey's girl friend on their last visit. His jaws champed on it. His voice, at any rate, was softened by the grape.

"Only two villains likely to have done it, if they're locals, are the Clint brothers. Nobody else for miles around. This is West Sussex, not the Smoke. Ever had dealings with 'em? They run a scrap yard . . . break up cars mostly . . . over by Harting."

"Never heard of 'em. I don't even know where Harting is."

Grout shrugged his wide flat shoulders. He asked a number of questions about

Beckworth's condition and his progress, ate two more grapes and left.

Progress was in fact slow. His memory came and went. His head healed well enough, and the rest of his body though it was black and blue for weeks where the boots had gone in, though strangely enough no bones had been broken.

"I'm too fat," he told Garvey. "They sunk their toe caps in it."

"Good thing, Len. But you won't be time you get out of here. You miss your beer, I guess."

Beckworth still had no clear memory of Miss Tatchell, nor of finding her dead poodle, though Garvey had told him of it. The newspaper man had now got into the habit of looking after Beckworth's garden for him and called regularly at the bungalow. He had also been keeping an eye open for Miss Tatchell's return but had seen no sign of her.

Again it was a comparative chance that brought back Beckworth's memory of the lady. This was a visit from Colonel Trivett and his wife one afternoon.

"Passing y'know," the colonel mumbled as if he had to excuse himself. "Thought we'd look you up. This is my wife."

Beckworth remembered the old colonel and the fact that he had never met his wife before. He could recall that her name was Agnes though he didn't know how he had learnt as much. He thought she was more like the popular idea of a farmer's wife with her dumpy figure and rosy cheeks than the usual picture of a colonel's lady as a stringy woman dried out by life in the tropics.

The colonel brought the conversation round to Miss Tatchell, and Beckworth said:

"I'm afraid you'll have to fill me in a bit, sir. There are some big void patches in my memory and Miss Tatchell's right in the middle of one."

So the colonel started going over events up to Miss Tatchell's departure, and quite suddenly it all came back to Beckworth. How he had met the old man at the gate to Orchard House; what he had been told;

his own subsequent searching of Tatch's desk and his later fruitless visit to Eastbourne. He saw again the colonel crouching over the carcass of the dog, and the old hall porter with the pebble glasses.

"Am I glad you called, Colonel! You've helped tremendously. It's mainly why I'm still here after so many weeks. My memory comes and goes like a dud TV set. But it's improving."

"Wondered if Tatch had been to see you?"

"No. Just as well, perhaps. I wouldn't have known her. Or maybe I would . . . can't tell with this damaged memory."

"She may not have known about the attack on you," Agnes suggested, "but she does now . . . that is if she's got my letter. She wrote to me from an hotel in Brighton, you know, and I replied asking them to forward my letter if she was no longer there."

"If you ask me," the colonel growled, "she's gone round the bend having come into so much money. She's still dodging around the countryside living in hotels to avoid publicity. Who the devil remembers it now? Anyway, we reckon we've seen the last of her in Funtingdon from the tone of her letter, eh, m'dear?"

"She said that she had seen a property outside Winchester she was thinking of buying," his wife supplied. "As soon as she has made up her mind she'll sell Orchard House. It really was an extraordinary letter. Not like the Tatch we know at all."

"There you are. What riches do for you, eh?" the colonel suggested.

Two days later Beckworth did in fact receive a letter from Miss Tatchell. By that time his memory of her was fully restored, and indeed he could recall everything of his life at Funtingdon since the day he had arrived there. He knew that he might wake up next morning to find gaps in it again but it was distinctly encouraging. He thought the day could not be far distant when he could leave hospital. The letter was strangely formal, and read as follows:

Dear Mr. Beckworth,

I was so sorry to learn of the attack upon you in the garden of your bungalow. I know that it happened some weeks ago but I have only just learnt about it. I do hope you are recovering well from the effects. I am sure you are because it is now some time since it happened. Whatever could have been the reason behind it, do you think? Had they intended robbery?

I am still doing my best to avoid the attentions of the Press. To do so I have to move continually from hotel to hotel though I am seldom inside them except to sleep. I know this must sound strange to you. I expect I have developed a phobia about it.

The other day I saw a very desirable property just south of Winchester, which I think I might buy rather than return to Funtingdon. If I do and settle there I will let you know and you must come and visit me. I know you have a key to Orchard House so perhaps you will be good enough to keep it till I have made up my mind about things when if needs be you can hand it over to the estate agents.

I do so hope you will soon be fully restored to health and will be able to leave hospital in the very near future.

Sincerely yours,
Tasmin Tatchell.

Beckworth showed the letter to Garvey when he made one of his periodic visits.

"Doesn't sound like Tatch at all," he said gloomily. "Read it. Could have been written by some prissy school marm or other."

Garvey read it and grinned.

"Yeah, strictly virginal, man. You remember her now? That's good, eh?"

Beckworth told him how the visit of Colonel and Mrs. Trivett had brought back his memory.

"That being so," Garvey announced, "I

can now tell you that the paper found Miss Tatchell staying in the Ship at Brighton. I went over there to speak to her."

5

"WHEN was this?" Beckworth demanded.

"Last . . . Tuesday, I think. Yeah, Tuesday. I saw you on the Monday. Would have told you earlier, made a special visit to do so if I'd known your memory of her had come back." Garvey produced a bottle of beer from the brief case, which he invariably carried to disguise the nature of the gifts he brought, and the sergeant found two glasses in his bedside cabinet. They opened the bottle and drank.

"I'm practically back to normal," Beckworth declared. "I'll be out of this place soon. How did you find Tatch? I mean . . . in herself. Opinions are that this inheritance has changed her completely."

"Well, she wasn't exactly the sort of dame I'd expected to find from your description of her character. Strictly funsville, you'd said. Outspoken. Called a spade a spade, and didn't give a damn for anybody, but good natured with it. That right?"

"Absolutely. In fact if there was one person to whom the sudden acquisition of a couple of million quid would have made no bloody difference whatsoever I would have said it was Tatch."

"Yeah. Well, in the first place she was up tight at having been found in the Ship. I had Susie with me . . . she's my pics girl, you know . . . and as soon as Tatch saw her camera she saw red as well. Practically threw her out . . ."

"Did you get a shot of her?"

"Nope. Might have hung around to snap her when she came out of the hotel, but the *Globe* don't encourage that sort of thing. You look at the paper you'll see that all pics are posed."

"Well?" Beckworth finished his beer, and wondered if Garvey had another bottle in the briefcase. He had.

"I calmed her down, but I got no real information out of her. Her plans were vague. All she was concerned about was keeping herself out of the limelight. She was thinking of buying another home, like she says in her letter."

Beckworth made no comment. He poured himself another beer and drank. Dark suspicions were forming in his mind.

"I've got to get out of here, Tom," he declared, "and when I do I don't want it publicized. The reverse in fact. Think you could print a few words to the effect that the ex-cop who was attacked in his garden looks like becoming a permanently bed-ridden hulk?"

"You think they'll have another go, Len?"

"I want 'em to think that I'm still in hospital when in fact I'm out and looking for 'em."

Garvey found another bottle in the recesses of his briefcase and topped up his own glass.

"Yeah, man, maybe it's time now your thinking box is fully restored we gave some thought to what it was all about." He drank deeply. "Those guys were waiting for *you*, Len. You, Leonard Beckworth, ex-detective sergeant CID, and nobody else. So why, man? To put you out of action for a long long time if not for good. They knew you were in the pub, and they waited. They weren't there to rob but to put you into hospital or into your box. How does that reasoning grab you, ex-Detective Sergeant Beckworth?"

"Pretty damn well." Beckworth fingered his face thoughtfully. Although now healed it had been tender to the touch for so long that testing it with his finger tips had become a habit. "I've got my own ideas about it, Tom. But there's precious little I can do in here except think, and I couldn't do much of that with an impaired memory. Jesus! I've lain in this blasted bed for weeks listening to the flies buzzing up and down the window and wondering if I'd ever do anything else. But last week full memory returned and God willing it'll stay that way. I need some physical therapy and then I'll be out. I won't rest till I've got the bastards who did it to me behind bars. Sergeant

Grout reckons that if they were local men it could have been two brothers name of Clint who keep a car breakers yard not far from a place called Harting. Think your paper will have their name on their files?"

"Likely, if they're ticketed crooks." Garvey made a note of the name. "I'll talk to our crime man."

"Another thing. No . . . forget it for the moment. It will have to wait till I'm out of hospital. Keep in touch, Tom, eh? I'd like you with me in Funtingdon as soon as I'm out."

"Sure, man. I'll call as soon as you're home."

Garvey had a number of questions to ask forming in his mind. For instance, if it had been two local crooks who had beaten up Beckworth, what had prompted them to do it? What was it that Beckworth had decided must wait till he was out of hospital? The newspaper man decided to shelve the questions for the time being, however. There was something inhibiting about a hospital room.

Beckworth had a further two weeks in hospital. During that time he had no more memory lapses and slowly built up his physical strength so that when he eventually emerged after being there nearly twelve weeks to the day he was as fit as he had ever been. He had lost over two stone in weight, and the doctors had advised him to keep it that way; advice that Beckworth felt sure that sooner or later would be forgotten however noble he thought it to be for the moment.

The bungalow, he found, had been kept in spotless condition by the indefatigable Mrs. Nash. Even the garden, now replete with the flowers and vegetables of high summer, was in good shape.

He had not been indoors long and was thinking about lunch in the Fox and Hounds when the door bell rang. It was Colonel Trivett.

"Glad to see you, Beckworth. Thought you might be home. Agnes said she saw a taxi turn in."

Beckworth took him into the lounge and poured him a military-sized gin. It was fairly obvious that not much went on in the road that escaped the notice of the Trivetts even though there might be hundreds of yards between houses.

"Heard any more of Miss Tatchell?" he asked idly.

"Not a word. I think she must be selling Orchard House. Saw some fellers working on the front door the other day. I asked 'em what they were doing. They said they'd come from Blackmores, the estate agents, and were changing the locks. One or two others in the village have heard from her including the vicar. She seems to have told 'em the same thing; that she was thinking of buying property outside Winchester and would be selling Orchard House. Extraordinary thing. I can't think what's come over the woman."

Beckworth made a non-committal reply, though he thought, grimly enough, that he knew what had come over her.

He had scarcely said goodbye to the colonel after walking to the gate with him when Garvey's yellow MGB hove into sight moving as usual as if the hounds of hell were on its tail, and crashing to its customary squealing stop.

Inside it in addition to its owner was his girl friend and photographer Susan Blakeney, who was nursing a picnic basket. She also had a square case holding her cameras and equipment. Behind her was a big black Alsatian dog, which leapt out barking furiously and charged towards Beckworth.

"Jesus H. Christ!" he blasphemed luridly and preparing to defend himself, "what is it? A Siberian Wolfhound?"

"Just a black Alsatian," Garvey grinned. "Name of Satan. I got him from a pal of mine. I thought you might like to have him around. Man, at first sight he'd scare the horns off his namesake, but that's about all he will do. Friendliest beast you ever met. Try him."

Beckworth put out a nervous hand to stroke the sleek head. The Alsatian's tail went round in circles and it whimpered with delight.

"There you are! Good watch dog

though. Frighten off a regiment. You've met Susie already. She's brought along a basket of goodies for lunch."

Seeing her for the first time whilst standing up on his own two feet Beckworth realized that she was not as tall as he had thought, barely up to his shoulder. She had short honey-coloured hair that had been artfully fanned out round her head. The sergeant, boorish in such matters, thought it looked like a chimney sweep's brush. But he had to admit that she was a pretty girl with wide and bright blue eyes, not to mention a beautifully shaped mouth. She was slim. In dress she was almost identical with Garvey. Both were in well-worn jeans and matching T-shirts with Globe printed across them. The ensemble, however, looked altogether shapelier on the girl.

Beckworth didn't really want the dog. It might prove a nuisance and it would be a responsibility of a sort he would sooner be without. But he was reluctant to tell Garvey as much. Jeeze, he thought, I'm a changed man all right. A year ago I would have told him what to do with the damned animal. It must be three months in hospital. That sort of experience makes a man humble.

"I've done my best, which is a para in the paper, to let everybody know that you're still in a hospital bed and likely to be there for a long long time," Garvey told him, while the girl was preparing lunch for them, "but if the two guys who attacked you were the local baddies . . . what did you say Grout said their name was?"

"Clint. They're brothers."

"Twins in fact. I talked to old Jim Starkey our crime man about them. They were done for robbery with violence ten years ago. They got eight and were inside for five. They're about thirty-two years old now. Starkey reckons that Sergeant Grout could be right about them being the guys who attacked you, but . . . and it's a big but, Len . . . this *is* West Sussex. It ain't exactly a resort of criminals. In consequence whenever violence of that nature *does* occur then the cops plump for the Clint brothers."

"Grout's no fool," Beckworth put in, "but it's proof he'll need. Of course he'd plump for the Clints."

"And that's my point. If it *was* them they might have been keeping an eye on this place to see if you're back and to have another go if you are. Hence, the dog. You got a gun, Len?"

Beckworth laughed.

"As you've just pointed out, this is West Sussex. It ain't America nor even South Africa. Of course I haven't got a gun."

"I thought so. I've got a sword stick you can have. It's in the car. I'll fetch it."

Garvey went out. The dog made no attempt to follow him though it scrambled to its feet. It looked enquiringly at Beckworth then came and sat at his feet to nudge his leg with its nose.

Garvey came back with the sword stick and they went into the garden for him to demonstrate its use. The thin steel blade flashed from its cane casing and whirled round him darting in and out as wicked looking as a serpent's tongue.

"Try it," he suggested. "Only danger is that it might stick in the cane just when you need it in a hurry. I've kept it greased with a silicon spray and it should be OK."

Beckworth because he thought that he would never be called upon to use it in earnest made a few half-hearted passes in the air. These called forth a frenzied barking from the dog, shrieks of laughter from the girl who was watching from the kitchen window, and ribald comments from Garvey.

"Christ, man! You look like a priest splashing the holy water around. That's a sword you've got. Put some guts behind it!"

The girl had an appointment after lunch for some photographic work and Garvey was aware that he had still not heard from Beckworth why the sergeant had specifically asked him to call. But the sight of the girl's camera case had given Beckworth an idea.

"If I set it up could you photograph some fingerprints for me?" he asked her.

"Sure. I always carry a selection of lenses."

He found some old face powder of his sister's and a scent spray which could be used for dusting the powder evenly over a shiny surface. The chopper that had killed Miss Tatchell's poodle was still wrapped in brown paper in Beckworth's tool shed. He set it up in the garage using the vice on the work bench. One very large thumb print and rather smudgy fingers on the opposite side of the handle came up well. Susan had no bother in photographing them and promised to let him have the prints next day.

Beckworth hinted that she should not talk to anybody about the prints or how he had come by them. She replied in Garvey's quaint turn of phrase but with a charming smile:

"Sure, man. Strictly mumsville, that's me. As Baldwin said, 'My lips are sealed'."

Beckworth gaped at her. Where on

earth had she learnt of Baldwin? He couldn't remember the prime minister himself.

Garvey was curious.

"A dog is a dog, is a dead dog," he said. "What gives?"

"You'll see. When you've dropped off Susie can you come back?"

"Not till much later. Hell, man! The paper does require my services from time to time."

"Fine!" Beckworth grinned. "If it's after dark so much the better."

When the couple finally departed the Alsatian made no attempt to follow them to the car. It seemed by some uncanny prescience to have determined that Beckworth was its new owner and dozed happily in the sun on the bungalow's porch. Beckworth left it there and went inside to put his own feet up for an hour or so.

Garvey returned at nine o'clock. By that time Beckworth had got home from the pub where he had taken the dog with him. There was no doubt that if anybody still aimed to make another attack upon him the big dog would make an admirable deterrent, peaceful as a lamb though it was in character.

"So here I am," the newspaper man announced. "What's on your mind, Len?"

"I'm going along to Miss Tatchell's house and I want you with me. You'll know why when we get inside it."

Beckworth during the course of his career had acquired a selection of skeleton keys which he had often used unofficially in the interests of crime detection. They were his property and he had not parted with them upon retirement.

"They've changed the locks at Orchard House," he told Garvey, stowing the bulky ring of keys into a pocket.

"They?"

"Estate Agents acting on Miss Tatchell's instructions presumably."

"Yeah, but why d'you want me there, man?"

"You'll see. Let's take the hound, eh? He'll give us warning if we're disturbed."

Garvey remembered that he had a lead for the dog in the car which he had intended handing over along with tins of Satan's favourite dog food. He went and fetched them.

There was nobody around when they reached Orchard House. The night was misty and chill. The moon a circle of blurred light in the eastern sky.

The new lock on the front door . . . the back one was bolted on the inside . . . succumbed easily enough to Beckworth's selection of skeletons. He took Garvey into the lounge. The electricity was switched off at the mains and he had to rely upon a hand torch for illumination. He swept the beam of this along the mantelpiece over the wide fireplace and settled it upon a large coloured photograph in its centre. The picture was one of Tatch's smiling face and very handsome she looked too with her big brown eyes enhanced by long lashes from the photographer's art and her generous nicely shaped mouth.

"That, Tom," Beckworth declared

seriously, "is Miss Tasmin Tatchell. What I want to know is this. Was she the woman you interviewed in a room at the Ship Hotel in Brighton?"

Garvey made his customary catch of breath when startled but burst out immediately:

"Christ, no, man! Nothing like her. The dame I saw had blue eyes for a start."

6

BECKWORTH nodded.

"What I thought," was all he said.

"Yeah, man," Garvey cried excitedly for he had seen in a moment the possibility of a sensational story behind the discovery, "but this could mean . . ."

"More than one thing, Tom. Let's get back to the bungalow, eh? We'll discuss it over supper. I did some shopping this afternoon."

His purchases included further supplies of York ham from a delicatessen in the city. Both of them ate generously of this. The dog sat between them ears cocked and eyes anxious for tidbits.

"First thing to consider," Beckworth declared, "is the possiblity of there being two Tasmin Tatchells, which is unlikely. The one you saw didn't deny the inheritance, I suppose? She didn't say, 'You've got the wrong woman'?"

"Not a chance. She even mentioned buying a new property like she said in her letter."

"So she's a substitute." Beckworth paused to fork up more ham and to champ on it. "Next thing to consider before we start thinking the worst is this," he continued, "has she assumed the role and is moving around from hotel to hotel registering in the name of Tasmin Tatchell on the orders of Tatch herself?"

"Hadn't thought of that," Garvey admitted ruefully. "I suppose she must be, come to think of it. I mean . . . the substitute ain't writing the letters, is she? Some one must know Tatch's handwriting."

"That could have been taken care of. The letter she wrote me was certainly not Tatch now I know there's another dame masquerading in her place. Besides . . ." Beckworth pointed a knife at Garvey, ". . . don't lose sight of what had me wondering in the first place: the death of her poodle, which was killed because it could have been a flaming nuisance to those responsible."

"I'm losing you, man," Garvey protested. "You reckon there's a plot afoot to rob the woman of her inheritance? This substitute is part of it?"

"If she's not working on Tatch's own orders, that's exactly what I think."

"But . . . hell, Len, man! How can they do it . . . get their hands on the bread? It's all tied up . . . protected by banks and solicitors."

"Maybe, but if you ask me what we're seeing is a long-term plot to rob Tatch of the money. Somebody knew, a long time before she did maybe, that old Beamish, her uncle, was worth five million and proposed leaving the bulk of it to his niece. So he had time to prepare, to find a substitute to masquerade in Tatch's place while they wait for probate . . . because that's what they're waiting for, Tom . . . while the substitute practises Tatch's handwriting and her signature, specimens of which they made it their business to obtain beforehand."

Garvey drank deeply of his bottled beer and gulped.

"What's happened to the real Miss Tatchell then?"

Beckworth cut fiercely across the last piece of ham on his plate so that the knife's edge squeaked.

"Dead, of course," he declared.

"Christ, man! You frighten me. You really do. But this is going to make one hell of a story."

"Not yet it ain't. There's just a chance that Tatch is still alive. After all it must be nearly as difficult to get rid of her body so that it's not found over a long period of time as it is to keep her a prisoner and alive somewhere. So we tread carefully, Tom. Your paper can help."

"How?"

"You've got agents in the States. Get me all the dope you can on the inheritance. When is it likely to be paid over and how. The Yanks are not so . . . how can I put it? . . . reticent in giving information."

Garvey nodded and glanced at his watch.

"I'll get a telex out tonight. But we had a certain amount from them concerning old Beamish when he died and the news broke that his money had been left to his niece. I made notes before I went along to the Ship in Brighton to see Miss Tatchell . . . the blue-eyed substitute that is." He paused to grope in his pocket and bring out a notebook. He flicked over the pages to refresh his memory. "The old boy arrived in the States about 1923, and led a bum's life till 1935 when he settled in Rockwall County, Texas. He bought a poultry farm there. During the war oil was discovered on neighbouring land. He let the chicken farm slide and worked on the oilfields. Local geologists convinced him there was oil under his own land, but it was not till 1976 when the energy crisis came along and improved techniques for drilling at greater depths were available that lifting it became a practicable proposition."

Garvey paused. Beckworth seemed to be unconcernedly finishing his supper so the newspaper man said:

"Want any more?"

"What have you got?"

"He became a USA subject in 1937 and married a woman called Louisa Frances Coltard the same year. She died in 1972. No kids. Beamish tried to trace her relatives using a well-known firm of private investigators but without success. Hell, Len! Most of this was printed over here in the reports . . ."

"I know, but I didn't read 'em. Any more on the actual inheritance?"

"Well," Garvey went on after consulting the notebook again, "the old boy hadn't the capital to raise the oil himself so he sold out for a reputed five million dollars to COP, Consolidated Oil Products, that is. He received a hundred thousand in cash and the balance in COP stock." He snapped the notebook shut. "That about wraps it up, Len. Shortly after the sale of his oil rights the old chap became a cancer patient. He was then eighty years old and set about finding any relatives he had left in England using a firm of Dallas attorneys. They found Miss Tatchell."

"Yeah, so did others apparently," Beckworth commented drily. "The more you consider the facts the more they match the idea that the substitute is part of a plot and not acting under Tatch's orders. The dead poodle. As I said it could have been an infernal nuisance even if they had put it in kennels. They were not to know that Tatch had a nosey old cop as a neighbour and expert in spotting disturbed soil. Nobody who knows or is acquainted with the real Tatch seems to have seen her since she left home . . ."

"You think she was taken . . . kidnapped I suppose you'd have to call it . . . soon after she left home?" Garvey put in.

"Must have been."

"You could check with Larkin, her

solicitor. Wasn't he there when she left in a taxi?"

"So he was, but I'm not calling upon Mr. Bloody Larkin again," Beckworth declared. "The leak of information concerning Tatch's affairs must have come from his office. I called there in the morning of one day and on the evening of the next I was clobbered in my own garden. That ain't bad going for West Sussex. Somebody was able to pick up a phone and say, 'Miss Tatchell has a nosey ex-cop as a neighbour living at Splitlevel Cottage. Get rid of the bastard'."

Garvey grinned.

"Doesn't that suggest, if it was as easy as you say, that whoever it was had already had dealings with the two who beat you up? Man, they could have been used to kidnap Miss Tatchell. Could have been the Clint brothers."

"Possibly. I'll investigate them in good time. But we've got to step carefully, Tom. If Tatch is not already dead then there is a fair chance she will be as soon as the people who've kidnapped her realize they've been rumbled. Do your best to find out from the States through your paper when probate on Beamish's will can be expected because it seems to me a further likelihood that if they ain't slit the lady's throat yet they will as soon as they've got the money."

"Could've got it already," Garvey suggested gloomily. "Hell, man, probate might not take long if it's straightforward work. Only if he left a lot of real estate would it take months." He glanced at his watch "I'd better get going and send that telex. They're about six hours behind us. What will you do, Len?"

"Tonight? Nothing. In the morning provided your girl friend has 'em ready I'll get Sergeant Grout to check on those finger prints with CRO. It could help."

"Meaning they might belong to one of the Clints?" Garvey asked. "If they do that's proof positive they're tied in with the kidnapping."

"We'll see."

Beckworth was too old a hand to commit himself.

True to her word Susan called at the bungalow with the prints early next morning as Beckworth was finishing his breakfast. She had driven over from Chichester using one of the Globe's small vans. The dog welcomed her as warmly as Beckworth did. The photograph of the thumb print was particularly clear and good.

"That'll do fine, Susie," he said enthusiastically.

She stared at him with her blue eyes serious and when she spoke it was without the usual flippancy.

"Do you think you ought to go on with this, Len?" she asked.

"You mean trying to find the men who beat me up and looking for Miss Tatchell? Why the hell not?"

"Len," she cried, "you've just spent three months in hospital. They nearly killed you! Don't you think that's enough?"

111

"I'm forewarned now. That's different."

She continued to stare at him wonderingly. Quite suddenly she grabbed him round the shoulders and kissed his cheek.

"For God's sake take care of yourself then. Don't you realize that we've grown quite fond of you, Tom and I?"

Then she was gone skipping down the bungalow's drive to the parked van leaving him with a hand to his cheek where she had kissed him bewildered by the thoughts chasing through his mind because it was something that had not happened to him in twenty years.

He left the dog in the garden when he drove into Chichester and found himself wondering if the animal would be all right left to its own devices, or if it might not run off.

"Christ!" he said to himself, "I'm getting soft."

Detective Sergeant Grout was in his usual pessimistic mood though Beckworth in getting this impression of the man thought it might be his gaunt lowering looks that were responsible for most of it. Grout said he would send the prints on to the CRO. He brightened a little when Beckworth explained quite untruthfully how he had come by them.

"Found an old chopper out of place on the floor of my garden shed when I got out of hospital. It was tidied away in a rack before I went in and I wondered if one of the guys who attacked me had been nosing around, looking for a handier weapon maybe, before I happened along. Anyway it carried dabs, which sure as hell are not mine because I've never used it. I raised 'em and had 'em photographed. Thought they might belong to one of the brothers you mentioned . . . Clint, wasn't it?"

"Sounds promising," Grout admitted. He said he would telephone Beckworth if he heard anything.

In the city, because he felt sure that it was from the office of Larkin, Brown and Larkin that the information necessary to the plot against Miss Tatchell had been leaked, Beckworth walked cautiously with an eye open for any passer-by who might recognize him. He was supposed to be in hospital, and whilst he was completely ignorant of the man or men responsible for putting him there they must surely know him even if he was now considerably thinner.

His destination was Carrs Bank in East Street where Miss Tatchell kept an account. He was well aware that all banks were exceedingly close mouthed about a customer's affairs, and rightly so, but there was a chance that he could get confirmation of what he was guessing had happened, and if he did it would clinch matters, and dispel any faint doubt in his mind of what had become of Miss Tatchell.

Carrs branch in East Street was a busy one. He quite expected to be told that the manager could not see him without an appointment but he let them know that he was Detective Sergeant Beckworth and the mention of his police rank was sufficient to earn him an appointment in twenty minutes time; a wait that never bothered him at all.

The bank's premises dated from Victorian times and the manager's room when at last he was shown into it had panelled walls and a high ceiling supporting an ornate chandelier so that Beckworth fully expected the manager, whose name was Wooley, to be an old gentleman with drundeary whiskers. In fact he was a young man in his thirties as slick looking as a car salesman in a well-cut dark lounge suit with an impeccably white collar and shirt, who shook hands with him gravely.

Beckworth told him that none of Miss Tatchell's neighbours had seen her since the news of her inheritance had hit the headlines. He told him truthfully that he knew she was a customer of his bank and added, untruthfully, that he had been deputed by her neighbours because he was an ex-policeman and a natural for the job, to come along and to ask him if he had any knowledge of the lady's present address. Her neighbours, of whom, he

Beckworth was one, were worried about her.

Mr. Wooley nodded as if in complete agreement with the neighbours' solicitude and said:

"Normally, as you doubtless know, I would not be prepared to give a stranger, even if he is a police detective sergeant, any information at all about a customer unless he first produced a court order, but in this instance, Sergeant, I see no objection to telling you that the lady has transferred her account to another bank in the city. So, I'm sorry, I can't help you."

"Do you mind elaborating on that, sir?"

"In what way? You want to know where the account is now?"

"Not so much where it is, sir. How was the transfer done? I mean how did she give you instructions? Did she give them to you in person, or did she write?"

"Why do you want to know that, Sergeant?"

Beckworth wished that young Mr. Wooley would not be so bloody cautious.

Hell! The account had gone so what had he to worry about?

"I'm curious, sir," he stated baldly. "She left home to dodge publicity and as far as we know has not been near the place again. She seems to have been infected with a sort of mania for privacy. I wondered if this applied to her relationship with her bank?"

Mr. Wooley pursed his lips in a sort of deliberation before replying:

"As a matter of fact, Sergeant, you may well be right about this horror of publicity that came over her when she inherited great wealth, though at the time when we transferred the account she had not as far as I know touched a penny of it. But I can only think it was why she transferred the account. People knew she banked with us. Therefore she must move the account. That seemed to be her reasoning."

He lined a paper knife up alongside his blotter's edge with extreme care then went on:

"I received her instructions to transfer

the account to the Southern County Bank in South Street. The instructions were written on Southern County's notepaper, and properly signed, of course. I was a bit put out I don't mind telling you because she'd had no reason to complain of our service and I drove out to Funtingdon hoping to see her, but, as you will appreciate, she was not at home. I know Mr. Sharp, the manager of Southern County's branch, and telephoned him. He was very apologetic. There was nothing he could do about it. She simply walked in there one morning four weeks ago and told him that she wished to transfer her account from this bank and branch to his. He gave her a piece of his notepaper and told her how to word the instruction. He was not particularly worried about a reference because the lady said she had been given to understand that her solicitors banked with him." Mr. Wooley shrugged. "I told him that in any event she had kept a satisfactory account with us, and that was that."

Beckworth thanked him and left. As he went through the front doors of the bank the thought occurred to him that perhaps he ought to have asked the manager how carefully he had checked the signature on the instruction to transfer. But young Mr. Wooley would have undoubtedly asked countless questions and at that stage Beckworth wanted himself and his suspicions completely in the background. The transfer of the account and the way it had been done was confirmation enough of his fears. He thought that the real Miss Tatchell must be dead but while there was the faintest chance that she was alive he was going to proceed very carefully indeed.

7

THAT night Beckworth awoke to hear the dog barking frenziedly. He scrambled out of bed, grabbed the sword stick and hurried into the hall where the dog had gone from its bed in the kitchen. When he opened the front door Satan bounded out and down the drive, his noise diminishing with distance. Beckworth listened carefully for further noises, in particular the sound of a car starting up. The night was chilly with a sliver of moon that had long disappeared in the west leaving only a hazy starlight through which he could distinguish nothing with certainty.

The dog's barking stopped and presently he came back head down and tail wagging apologetically. The incident proved nothing. The dog took advantage of the situation to sleep on the bottom of Beckworth's bed comfortably warm and heavy against his feet for the remainder of the night. His presence there in the morning served as a reminder of what might have happened had the animal not frightened off what could have been some intruders. Satan could have sensed the presence of a fox outside, nothing more, but Beckworth saw again the raised clubs against the moon, heard the hoarse breathing of his attackers and smelt their acrid stink of desperation as he had fought them. He recalled Susan Blakeney's words. *They nearly killed you*. Wasn't it time he bowed out? What the hell was Miss Tatchell to him? He liked her but she was really nothing more than a neighbour. Ought he not to pass his suspicions on to Sergeant Grout of the local CID and leave it at that?

He thought about it for a long time but knew that he could never drop it. He was not sure that he had sufficient to offer the local boys to ensure that they followed it up. And if they did might it not endanger Tatch's life? That is, if she were still alive, which he doubted. Besides he had been brutally attacked by two men and that had hurt him mentally as well as physically because he was a cop with a loathing for villains that had given him a pride the two thugs had shattered. He wanted to find them and to get back at them. It was easy to tell himself to wait till he heard from Grout about the finger prints before making another move. Maybe they belonged to one of the Clints, then he would know where to go.

But the prints did not belong to either of the Clints. It was three days before Grout telephoned him, his honking voice clattering loudly in the earpiece.

"Didn't you say you got those prints off a chopper in your garden shed?" Grout demanded.

"That's right."

"Well, there's something screwy going on here or I'm a monkey's uncle. They belong to a guy named Bishop. Arthur Henry Bishop."

"So?" Beckworth asked.

"What in the name of Jesus was this bloke doing in your woodshed?" Grout wailed. "He's a solicitor, or was a solicitor, struck off the List or the Rolls, or whatever they call 'em after conviction for embezzlement. He milked his Clients' Account. Got four years and came out in 1975. I mean . . . it's screwy. What's the answer, Sergeant?"

"How the hell do I know?" Beckworth bawled back. "It's not my shed, or it is now. I inherited it from my sister. But the prints have been under cover and could have been made months ago. Maybe she knew him and he chopped a bit of wood for her sometime. Thanks for trying, anyway. Better let me have his description while you're about it. Could be the guy has sunk so low in the social scale he's taken to beating up ex-cops for a living. The size of the thumb print suggests he's got the build for it."

"You can say that again," Grout declared. "He's a bloody giant. Six feet four. Weighs 240 pounds. Eyes dark brown. Sallow complexion. I've got his picture here. Long face. Black hair. Hey, what d'you know? Against Peculiarities they've typed, 'Has an affected mode of speech.' What does that mean, for Pete's sake?"

But Beckworth was beyond giving speculative answers. He said: "Thanks a lot, Sergeant," and hung up.

Deacon!

The name had been ringing in his head from the moment he had heard the description. It couldn't have required any deep thought on the part of Arthur Henry Bishop to choose another ecclesiastical title when looking for a pseudonym before getting the job of managing clerk with Larkin, Brown and Larkin, doubtless with the aid of forged references. Did Charles Larkin know that his clerk was an ex-solicitor dethroned because of embezzlement? Beckworth couldn't see that it mattered for the moment. Deacon had killed Tatch's poodle. It was not all that surprising, perhaps, because he had been at Orchard House when its owner had left but once you knew the man to be an ex-convict then all manner of possibilities became apparent. Deacon could have known about Miss Tatchell's inheritance months ahead of the event. Indeed she had been advised by her solicitors obviously informed in turn by the Dallas attorneys that her old uncle had made her his heir. Deacon could have realized then that no American firm acting on behalf of a client who was then eighty years old and dying, would have been given instructions to trace a relative in England unless the client had a great deal more than an itty bitty chicken farm to leave behind.

Lone spinsters are always fair game for villains looking for a victim to pluck and Tatch had been no exception. Doubtless she had at one time had occasion to write to her solicitors and the letter had been in their files waiting for Deacon to extract and to hand to the woman he had found to play the role of substitute so that she could take her time over learning the writing and practising the signature. The substitute was obviously something like Tatch in build, and possibly voice, though the blue eyes were a dead give away. But you can't have everything,

Beckworth thought. Provided the substitute took care to keep clear of the real Miss Tatchell's haunts, and flitted from hotel to hotel, keeping up the impression of a sudden desire for privacy, putting it about in writing to acquaintances that she would never return to Funtingdon, then the plot was on the high road to success. Transfer of the banking account had been achieved. All they were waiting for was probate and the transfer of the cash.

But Beckworth remembered Garvey's gloomy remark that perhaps they already had it. He worried over this and decided that if he were Deacon with millions to be filched once he had his hands on it or had achieved its transfer to his own name he would be high tailing it towards an airport and the safety of a country where thieving rogues were generally welcome.

Beckworth decided that he must check on Deacon without delay. He reached for the telephone directory, looked up the number of Larkin, Brown and Larkin, and then dialled it. A girl answered and he said:

126

"Is Mr. Deacon there?"

"Hold on a moment, please."

When Deacon's unmistakable voice announced, "Mr. Deacon here," Beckworth cut off. It might make the man suspicious but that couldn't be helped, nor was there any guarantee that because the man was still in the country he had not yet collected Tatch's inheritance. He ought really to find out all he could about the solicitor's clerk. His private address for instance. The man's associates if he had any. Where he went and whom he saw. If Tatch were alive then Deacon might lead him to the place where she was being kept. When he saw Garvey that evening they would have to try to arrange a stake out on Deacon even if it meant employing others to keep a twenty-four hour watch on him. In the meantime, Beckworth decided, he could make a start himself.

It was child's play to follow the big man home. He was completely unsuspecting though Beckworth thought he should have been cautious after a mysterious caller on the telephone that morning had cut off having established his presence in the office.

Deacon lived in Pagham in a small bungalow as alike the others in the road as its builder's bricks. Beckworth had seen him leave the office in North Pallant and collect his car, a blue Marina, from a nearby car park. He had followed it to Pagham and stopped well down the road as soon as its indicators showed that it was turning in to one of the bungalows.

Beckworth's field glasses were ready to hand. He saw Deacon bring the car to a halt against the garage doors, get out and be greeted by a well proportioned woman with a wifely kiss. He couldn't see the colour of her eyes but could she be not only Deacon's wife but the substitute Miss Tatchell? Why not? He must get Garvey to take a look at her.

After the couple had gone indoors Beckworth waited five minutes then started up again and drove slowly past noting the number of the Deacon's abode. It was a start.

Garvey and Susan were due for supper that night. Beckworth was expecting the reporter to have further details of the inheritance from America but in fact he had not yet received a reply to his telex.

"Swell, man," Garvey exclaimed when he had been put in the picture concerning Deacon. "We know his place of business and his home address. The bastard can't be in both at the same time. I reckon we can watch him for eighteen hours out of the twenty-four without roping in extra labour. You employ private eyes for instance they'll cost a mint. Either Susie or me will contrive to get a look at Mrs. Deacon. If she's been playing the substitute, Len, that will just about clinch it. In fact, once we've identified her as the woman we saw in the Ship at Brighton claiming to be Miss Tasmin Tatchell you can go to the cops and hand the whole job to them on a platter."

"Not so fast," Beckworth growled. "I don't even know if the woman *is* Mrs. Deacon. If she's not he could deny all knowledge of her. I daresay the two of them have worked out some dandy plan whereby they'll disappear quick as startled lizards once they're rumbled. Besides, I daren't lose sight of the chance of Tatch being alive somewhere. Deacon could lead us to her."

The girl had been preparing supper. With the last dishes and plates on the table she sat down herself. Garvey reached for the Stilton while she cut bread.

"So brother Deacon has been in the Nick, has he?" he said. "What if he met up with the local villains, the Clints, while he was there? How does that grab you, Len? It would explain how soon he was able to whistle up assistance to put you out of action after you first called upon Larkin."

"So it would," Beckworth agreed. He helped himself to another glass of beer pouring it expertly to avoid getting too much of a head on it. "If he was done for embezzlement and they were done for robbery with violence it's not likely they finished in the same jug. But it's possible," he went on. "The interesting bit is that it was done so quickly. I mean a man like Deacon and from what I've heard of the Clints, they'd be poles apart normally even if they had been cell mates at one time. How long ago I'd have to guess, but it was something like four years. Now how the hell do you get into touch with the Clints after that time? Not only that how do you get them to agree to do a job for you; a job which if they were caught would put 'em back in the Nick a damned sight quicker than they came out? How do you agree a price, find the money to pay it perhaps, all within a few working hours?"

"Unless," Garvey suggested. "They've already done a job for you quite recently; a job like kidnapping Miss Tatchell."

Beckworth finished his beer. He helped himself to bread and buttered it almost absent-mindedly.

"I think," he said carefully, "that I must pay the Clints a visit. First thing in the morning. How the hell do I find 'em?"

"Susie knows. She's been there."

"Well, sort of," the girl corrected him. "They run a scrap metal business. It's nothing but a used car dump really situated off the B road between Chichester and Petersfield before you get to Harting. It's way out. Has to be I guess. It's an eyesore. I suppose it was a small holding originally."

"You had business with them?" Beckworth asked.

She laughed.

"Not a chance. There used to be an old Manor House and estate there called Farmfield Manor. The house has been pulled down and the estate's become farm land. You can bet the Clints would never have been able to turn their bit into a car dump if the old baron was still living there. I went out there to take pics for the Globe. There's a big lake there that has thermal qualities. You know, the water's warm. The Ministry of Energy were interested and the SEB were doing some experimental work extracting heat

132

from the water. The Globe did an article on it."

"SEB?" Beckworth asked.

"Southern Electricity Board to you."

When they had gone and before going to bed Beckworth looked at his road map. It was a few years old and Farmfield Manor was marked on it. He decided against taking the dog. One of the animal's most useful characteristics was that it never seemed to resent being left on its own. He thought he would make an early start.

8

BECKWORTH enjoyed the drive. The road to Petersfield, after leaving the Midhurst one out of Chichester, ran straight for the mouth of a valley through the South Downs with rolling farm lands on either side. It was already beginning to shimmer under the heat of the early September sun. When the hills closed in the land became wooded. The road narrowed, climbed and twisted bringing him to open fields again. He slowed the car. Somewhere along here was the track he had seen on the Ordnance map which would take him to the remains of Farmfield Manor. Along this the Clints' place was located.

A crudely painted sign on a wilting board stuck in the side of the track pointed the way with a barely decipherable arrow and the words: "Car Dump". It was really better than a track, macad-

amized but with pot-holes galore. Beckworth drove down it slowly. He planned
to pass by the entrance to the dump, park
out of sight and return to reconnoitre on
foot. There was no sign of human habi-
tation. The lane, meandering between
high banks dense with sapling growth,
seemed to be leading nowhere.

The Clints' holding when he reached it
proved to be in a small valley. There was
just a plain two-storied house as square as
a toy fort at the side of the lane with bare
ground all round it. Behind on both sides
were lines of piled and wrecked cars,
dumped like crushed beetles one on top
of another, in lanes behind the square
house. As he passed Beckworth saw that
somebody was using an acetylene cutting
torch in the yard beside the house. He
caught a glimpse of the electric blue flame
and a shower of bright red sparks. There
was the jib of a mobile crane poking up
above the slates of the house, and two
small bulldozers with shining steel shovels
parked to one side. He guessed that most
of the work was done by the dozers

pushing the worthless remains of the wrecks around.

Past the house the lane climbed out of the shallow valley then dipped again. Without the traffic to and from the Clints' place the surface was weed-grown and the lane had narrowed with brambles reaching out to scratch at the passing car. Pretty soon it came to an abrupt end against a set of tall and rusted iron gates. The brick walls on both sides of them had long since crumbled into nettle-grown rubble and now the vertical rusty bars of the gates looked more like the side of a gigantic cage than the guardians of a stately home they once had been.

Farmfield Manor, Beckworth supposed. The drive behind the gates was barely discernible under the all-pervading grass. He looked for a vantage point from which he could spy upon the Clints' holding and decided that the side of the valley behind him was the best bet.

Beckworth took his field glasses from beneath the dash, decided at the last moment that it might be prudent to turn the car so that it pointed to the way back, did this, left it unlocked and struck off over the coarse grass, brown as desert dust after the summer's drought, towards the top of the valley's side.

He had been disappointed in his brief glimpse of the Clint house as he had driven past. The whole extraordinary place; the monumental graveyard of old cars dumped in a Sussex valley; an eyesore mercifully hidden away and doubtless a deciding factor in authority allowing its existence, had yet looked to be too active a place for them to be keeping a woman like Tatch in the house against her will. Odd lorries carrying wrecks must arrive there from time to time. Maybe the Clints did all the work themselves. The only skill required would be in using the acetylene torch for cutting up metal, but there must be women in the house as well if the Clints were married. Not easy to keep a person prisoner in it under such circumstances.

Beckworth, who had been buoyed up into believing he might find Miss Tatchell

137

by the idea of the Clints having been used in her abduction, felt his heart sinking. Tatch was dead. She must be.

His loss of weight made the walk to the top of the rise no effort for him but he was sweating under the September sun by the time he reached it. He settled himself on the rim of a dell where he could stretch flat and bring the glasses comfortably to his eyes.

There were three wrecks awaiting stripping of any serviceable parts he saw behind the house including the one a black overalled figure was working on with the acetylene torch. He assumed that once this had been done the wreck would be pushed away by one of the dozers and then lifted on to a pile by the crane. What the business needed, he thought, was one of those huge crushing machines that could reduce a car to a cubic yard of concentrated metal but the capital outlay required for its purchase was probably too much for the Clints to find.

He felt a sudden quickening of interest. Parked farther away beside a colossal heap of old tyres was an old Ford Zephyr, dark red in colour and well battered. He was unable to read the last letter of its registration number but he felt sure it was the car he had seen parked close to his bungalow the night he had been attacked.

So he had established that much if nothing else. Beckworth experienced the old contemptuous hatred of villains flooding his being again. God help the Clints if ever they had occasion to cross his path, or he could think up a way of getting back at them. Had they had anything to do with the abduction of Tatch? She was his present concern, not vengeance against two hired strong-arm men. He could keep observation for a bit then Deacon must be his target.

When it came to such work Beckworth's patience was well nigh inexhaustable. He watched the house and yard for an hour but saw nothing untoward. The man in black overalls continued cutting away at a wreck with his oxy-acetylene torch under a shower of glittering sparks. An old woman came out of the back door of the house to tip away a bucket of slops. A car drove into the yard. The fellow in overalls chatted to its driver for five minutes then the car pulled out again and drove away towards the main road. Nothing stirred between times. Larks sang high in a sky the colour of a hedge sparrow's egg and insects buzzed in the long yellow grass in which Beckworth was concealed.

He thought that before he gave up he ought to make a circuit of the property because the piled ranks of dead autos were high enough in places to conceal a low building from his sight viewed even from his present elevated spot.

Taking care to keep himself below the sky line Beckworth trudged over the grass towards the end of the lot. The ground rose slowly. When it dipped again he saw the end of the car dump and the Clints' holding. Lying flat again he wriggled himself into position to be able to see that there were no other buildings save the house on the site. The ground rose gently behind the lot. He could see no gate there but twin depressions in the rank grass betrayed the fact that a vehicle or vehicles had been driven from the dump and over the rise. Curious about this he moved forward again to be able to see what was beyond the higher ground.

The lake Susan had mentioned was on the other side. It had been fenced in and there was a cluster of single-storey concrete buildings at its eastern end. Beyond it he could make out the remains of terraced gardens, and the ruins of an old house. Huge oaks standing out like islands in a sea of ploughed acres showed where the park had once been.

Beckworth gave the scene little attention. He was more concerned with viewing the car dump from yet another angle though he was curious about the car tracks over the rise and down to the lake. They were little used he thought for the grass, though bent and broken, had not been worn down to bare earth.

Using a fold in the land so that for a brief few seconds only he could have been observed from the house Beckworth moved down to the back of the dump. He saw that the rear exit from the place was nothing but a gap in a fence, itself no more than two strands of rusted wire supported on rotting posts. A small ditch had been filled in where the fence was missing to give a vehicle passage.

Ever curious if not actually suspicious Beckworth walked cautiously into the dump and along the rutted earth between the piled wrecks. In many cases they were so badly crumpled he could not recognize the make. Most of them had wheels and headlights missing. Those with lamps appeared to be peering down at him with a sort of lopsided gravity as if accusing him of invading their privacy.

He was in what he thought was the central lane and very soon came upon wheel tracks off to his left. Following these he saw that an archway under the piled wrecks had been made of rough timber and parked inside this was a small rowing boat on a trailer. As Beckworth approached a rat flicked away from under it. The boat had a small outboard motor tilted on its stern but no oars nor anything else inside its dirty interior.

So this was responsible for the tracks over the hill behind the dump. The Clints, or perhaps their children, did some fishing in the lake. Doubtless this was not authorized which was why they took care to conceal the boat, but it was all completely innocuous.

Beckworth went back the way he had come after a few more cautious peerings along the lanes between wrecks, but when he was over the skyline he went down to the lake instead of back to his car.

When he reached it he was astonished to find that the fence he had observed earlier, which appeared to enclose the whole lake, was actually of quite formidable proportions, certainly proof against anybody but the most determined and well equipped intruder. It was of closely spaced iron railings curved outwards and spiked at their tops with a frieze of barbed wire and at least eight feet high. Its construction must have cost a fortune. The expenditure of so much money in this comparative wilderness was explained when Beckworth saw a notice attached to twin gates in the fence situated where the tracks reached the lakeside.

The notice read:

DANGER

Property of the Ministry of Energy. The water in this lake is used by the Southern Electricity Board in experiments in the conservation of energy. The Public is hereby warned against its use for fishing, boating or bathing, or any other purpose without due authorization. Trespassers will be prosecuted.

The gates, Beckworth observed, were secured at their middle by a stout chain joined by a large padlock. This, and the gates' hinges, had been liberally oiled and recently.

Inside the fence at this point was the cluster of low-roofed concrete buildings he had observed from afar. Fat black pipes came out of these at intervals and curved writhing like giant anacondas into the brown water of the lake. There seemed to be no sign of life except for the birds anywhere. Apart from the recent oiling of the gates Beckworth would have said that the place had been undisturbed for months.

A prodigious waste of the taxpayers' money was how he summed it up. Propping the field glasses against a gap between two of the fence's vertical rails he inspected the far corners of the lake. There was nothing about it to suggest that it contained odd properties of underground heat or whatever it was that had attracted the scientists and the expenditure of public money. The water certainly had a dark somewhat sinister look, but its fringes of reeds and small islands of water lilies were nothing out of the ordinary. Moorhens and coots were drifting happily on the placid surface.

Searching the banks through the glasses Beckworth decided that between himself and the extreme western end of the lake, where there was a copse of trees growing down to the water's edge, was a small island also overgrown with trees. The whole lake, he thought, was about eight hundred yards in length and five hundred yards across roughly in a giant oval, quite an expanse of natural water and doubtless what had prompted the first baron to build his manor overlooking it so many centuries ago. The island, he decided, must be comparatively close to the western bank. He had not noticed it when he had first seen the place from the rise between it and the Clints' car dump possibly because the elevation had not been sufficient. He could recall now having seen a recent programme on the Southern television on the possibilities of heating houses and flats in Southampton from natural heat obtained from the earth. The screen had shown a map of the area depicting a wide circle round the port in which this heat was available. The lake Beckworth supposed came within this area. But what would it cost to develop?

He thought he could detect the corner of a roof amongst the trees on the island.

When he had moved along the fence and brought the glasses to bear again he could see more of it but the building was a wooden hut with a tarred felt roof, pretty big but nothing like the concrete constructions at the eastern end of the lake. For one astonishing moment he thought he had detected movement amongst the trees of the island. A second later he was sure of it. He could see a figure moving hesitantly through the trees as if not sure of its way. It came out on the south bank. Beckworth thought there must be a chair or bench there because the figure sank slowly out of sight, again as if not sure of its movements.

He hurried round the fence stopping every now and again to check if he could see more with the glasses till he had the figure in full view. It was a woman in a brown jersey and slacks, her face already as tanned as an oak apple, lifted towards the sun. She was in a deck chair.

She was too far distant for him to be absolutely sure even through the glasses but she was a big generously proportioned woman and she had black glossy hair. His hands shook rattling the binoculars against the fence.

"Jesus Christ!" he said aloud. He had found Miss Tatchell.

9

AT the same time as Beckworth took the road towards the Clints' car dump Tom Garvey was arriving in Carlton Road, Pagham, which was where the Deacons' bungalow was situated.

As far as he was aware Garvey had nothing particularly urgent awaiting him in the way of duty on behalf of the *Globe*. The local rotary club had an important politician as the guest speaker at their monthly luncheon in the city and he was expected to attend in case by some chance the politician should say anything important, though it was a routine duty Garvey could skip if needs be. This was just as well because although he didn't know it events were going to crowd in on him to such an extent that the rotary club luncheon would not be given another thought.

He had decided that he might usefully fill in his time by checking whether or not the woman living with Deacon, and presumably his wife, had been the woman he had seen at Brighton posing as Miss Tasmin Tatchell.

He had reckoned on perhaps having a long and dreary wait in front of him to achieve this but in fact he was almost immediately successful. He had chosen a vantage point where he parked the MGB and had picked up his borrowed binoculars to focus them on the bungalow's green front door when activity showed. The door opened and the huge figure of Deacon emerged carrying two suitcases. He carried these to his car, the blue Marina, which had been parked in the drive facing the closed garage doors. He opened the boot and put in the larger of the two cases but left the other standing alongside. He then got in the Marina and backed it out to the roadway where he parked it again at the kerb. Deacon then went back to the garage, and opened its twin doors. Inside there was a red Mini.

He opened the back of this and slipped the remaining suitcase into it. He disappeared into the garage and presently a puff of exhaust showed that he had started the Mini. This too was backed out into the road and parked next to the Marina. Garvey was intrigued to think that the man had been able to squeeze his huge bulk into the tiny car and watched him get out of it with even more interest.

Deacon went back to the garage, closed its doors and locked them. He had scarcely done this when the woman came out of the house. She looked as if she were dressed for travelling. She was wearing a tweed costume, carried an outsize handbag and a light mac. As she walked along the front of the bungalow towards Deacon, Garvey was able to see her face quite clearly and recognized her immediately as the woman who had registered at the Ship as Miss Tatchell.

Garvey experienced a glow of satisfaction with this. It looked as if the woman was off on another jaunt somewhere to keep up the continuing saga of Miss

Tatchell as a woman suddenly and strangely smitten with a mania for dodging publicity though the need for this had long since departed. He saw her and Deacon embrace each other as ardently as any married couple then Deacon got into the Marina and drove off followed by the woman a minute later in the Mini. Neither of them so much as glanced at the shabby yellow MGB as they passed.

The newspaper man drove leisurely back to Chichester where he went round to his girl friend's digs in Festival Court. It was still comparatively early and he whiled away an hour or so drinking coffee and chattering with Susan before he reported into the Globe office. By then it was ten thirty and he had not been there five minutes before he was handed a copy of a telex from the Dallas Star in Texas. Garvey read it. His jaw dropped open, and he said, plaintively, "Oh, Christ!"

The telex ran as follows.

Reference your telex No. 568 of the 2nd signed Garvey. Probate on the will of Thomas Ralph Beamish was obtained on the last day of August. Estate consisted of roughly two hundred thousand dollars in cash and five million dollars in COP stock. No real estate. COP stock is made up of ten thousand dollar bearer bonds redeemable year 2,000. Interest at 10% payable by coupons attached due 30th June and 31st December each year. Beamish made bequests of one hundred thousand dollars each to Mr. and Mrs. Craig Swanton with whom he was living at the time of his death and the remainder to his niece Miss Tasmin Tatchell resident in England. Estate attracted death duties of roughly one and a half million dollars. We understand that the balance of COP stock was transferred to England on the third of the month by means of Chemical Bank, New York, twice weekly courier to their London office. Regret we were unable to inform you earlier for security reasons. We would appreciate photograph of Miss Tatchell if one is now available and an account of her reactions to the receipt of her fortune if possible though we are aware from earlier communications that she is a difficult subject. Thompson, Overseas Editor.

Garvey read the telex a second time but it failed to improve his reactions to it. Five days had gone by since the three and a half million dollars' worth of bonds had started on their journey, which would end presumably at Miss Tatchell's bank, or rather the pseudo Miss Tatchell's bank, in South Street. Were they already there, and perhaps more to the point, had they been collected by the woman purporting to be Miss Tatchell?

Garvey had contacts all over the city. In spite of a happy-go-lucky attitude towards life and a generally hippie-like appearance he was a shrewd enough young man when it came to gathering news. He had been successful in establishing contacts in the Festival theatre, the cathedral close, the main stores and businesses, the local institutions and even in the police but when he had tried to get them in the local banks he had failed utterly. His methods were frowned upon by some who considered them unethical because he thought nothing of handing out a fiver or so when necessary and this often paid off. Indeed if he had not bribed a distant neighbour of Miss Tatchell's to telephone him as soon as he saw anybody in or out of Orchard House he would never have met Detective Sergeant Beckworth retired, or learnt of his suspicions which Garvey felt sure were going to lead him eventually to a sensational scoop.

He pondered on the situation. The vision of Mrs. Deacon driving away in a red Mini with a suitcase in its back and the lady dressed in a way which suggested somehow that she was off on a journey of some duration arose in his mind.

He could recall how Beckworth had given him his opinion that once the Deacons had the inheritance in their possession they would be leaving the country. Now that he knew Miss

Tatchell's fortune to be in the shape of bearer bonds he saw how eminently practicable this made the actual theft of it to be. Deacon must have done his homework thoroughly and obtained all the details of the inheritance, the exact nature of the stock involved, long before Beamish had actually departed this world.

Garvey wondered how much the repeal of the Exchange Control Act had contributed to the decision to plunder Miss Tatchell's inheritance. Before its repeal he knew that the possession of bearer bonds by any individual in the United Kingdom was forbidden. They had to be lodged with a bank and kept in a bank. The bank itself had been forbidden to hand them over to an individual, even a non-resident, without the prior permission of the Control. Now all restrictions had gone. Even so Garvey could see how essential it would be for Deacon to get out of the country as soon as he had his hands on the bonds. No bank manager in the land, although legally he could do nothing but follow his customer's orders, was going to let a lady walk out of his office carrying a parcel of bonds worth three and a half million dollars without asking the most pertinent questions and when he might expect to see the bonds back safely in his strongroom.

In this instance, Garvey decided, the pseudo Miss Tatchell would have had the backing and authority of her solicitors behind her and would have probably thought up some plausible reason for needing the bonds for a short time. Indeed it was possible that she would ask the bank to send the bonds along to the solicitor's office where Deacon, with or without the knowledge of a partner, would be waiting to collect them. Garvey could not help recalling that he had seen Deacon put a suitcase into his own car. He reached for the telephone.

He had a contact in the city's principal travel agents. In this instance it was a girl. In his opinion she was not a bad looker and possessed a figure which he often pictured in his more erotic fancies. Her name was Honey Brook. She was on duty and Garvey wasted no time on preliminary chat.

"Honey, you're the one girl in the whole wide world who can help me, darling. Strictly business. What I need to know is whether or not some folks named either Deacon or Bishop . . . no, they're not parsons . . . far from it . . . those are surnames . . . have bought airline tickets recently to take them out of the country. I'd say South America somewhere, possibly Switzerland. They might not have booked through your agency but you could phone around for me, maybe? Ring me back, eh? Life or death, Honey."

"I'll see what I can do."

She did very well, for within twenty minutes she was back with the information that a Mr. and Mrs. Arthur Bishop were booked to leave Heathrow on a Swissair flight to Geneva that afternoon at fifteen hundred hours.

Bishop, Garvey thought, because the passports were in that name. But it was a fairly common one and the couple booked to fly out of Heathrow were not necessarily the villainous Deacons.

Garvey wished he had Beckworth with him, but he knew the sergeant had gone to look over the Clints' place. To chase after him and to find him in order to give him the news seemed an awful waste of what might prove to be valuable time. He would also have liked to have called upon the Southern County Bank in South Street to enquire if the COP bonds from America had reached them, and if so what had happened to them, but he knew that the bank would tell him in so many words to go boil his head rather than give him any information concerning a client.

He decided that the only action he could take would be to call upon Charles Larkin, the solicitor, at his office in North Pallant and to try to get some sort of reaction from him concerning what was happening to Miss Tatchell's inheritance. If he were to show Larkin a copy of the telex received from Dallas, for instance, that surely would be good enough in conjunction with the news that his managing clerk's wife had been posing as Miss Tatchell, for the solicitor to take notice.

The telex machine produced an original and two copies of any messages received, and taking a copy with him, Garvey went round to North Pallant. The journey, short as it was, yet gave him the opportunity for further thought on the subject of Larkin. Although he had heartily disliked the man on the only occasion he had met him Garvey was finding it difficult to see Larkin in the role of a villain. But he kept asking himself how the firm had come to employ a convicted man, qualified in law though he might once have been, in the first place, such as Deacon, who had been able to play ducks and drakes with a client's inheritance apparently without the sole active partner having an inkling of what had been going on. Well, obviously Deacon must have produced forged references when presenting himself for employment, and equally obviously these had not been followed up, which was bad enough in all conscience. It seemed to Garvey that if any excuse could be found for Larkin it was that since the death of Octavius Brown, he had been the only active partner and had been so overwhelmed with work that Deacon's shenanigans had gone unnoticed.

More alarm vibrated in Garvey's mind when upon reaching the door of the unpretentious entrance to Larkin, Brown and Larkin's offices he found it firmly locked. No amount of knocking or ringing produced a reply. What the hell was going on? Any worthwhile firm of solicitors kept its office doors open during normal business hours even if there were no partners available, and for all he knew they might be required to do so by law.

Enquiries of a neighbouring office were no help.

"Some of them were there first thing this morning," a receptionist told him, "because I saw Lisa Tarrant arrive. She's Mr. Larkin's secretary. They may have closed for a week's holiday. Why don't you try telephoning them? They're sure to have an answering service working. That might tell you something."

It told him nothing other than to leave his own telephone number when he would be phoned back as soon as possible. Uneasiness plucked at Garvey's mind leaving discord like the sound from an ill-used fiddle string. What to do next? The Deacons' suitcases and an aircraft leaving the ground loomed largely in his thoughts.

The telephone directory refreshed his memory of Charles Larkin's private address. He had known it before. Trees Court, a private estate south-west of the city close to Fishbourne. He was reluctant to telephone. The brush-off was too easy. After that, if Larkin were not at home, he would have to go on to try to find Beckworth.

It took him five minutes in the MGB to arrive at the entrance. It was like calling upon a country house which was in fact what Trees Court had once been. The old mansion had been pulled down and a sprawl of carefully sighted bungalows, so designed and located that each had a maximum view of the grounds and a minimum sight of its neighbour, had been put up in its place. There were communal tennis courts, a swimming pool, putting and croquet lawns for the sole use of owners.

"Snobsville," Garvey thought of it as he drove along the freshly minted asphalt looking for the individual driveway to No. 10. He passed the swimming pool, a shimmer of intensely blue water, so clean nobody could have so much as dipped a toe into it, or so it appeared. Certainly nobody was using it.

The front door to No. 10, and probably those of its neighbours, Garvey thought, was deeply inset at the end of a small fore-court. No neighbour could see you calling, not even your car if it were taken to the front door.

Larkin was not at home, though the front door was standing ajar. Again uneasiness nagged at Garvey's mind. What the hell did that mean? He rang and knocked several times before pushing the door open and stepping into the neat hall.

"Anyone at home?" he called uselessly.

Obviously there was not or his ring and knock would have been answered. Garvey should then have gone away, but he was first and foremost a newspaper reporter. There was news, sensational news in the shape of a stolen inheritance transcending all else in his mind and there was no room for the exercising of morals, ethics, or even manners to be considered in his search for the truth.

The hall's fitted carpet, biscuit coloured and of deep texture, enabled him to walk silently to a door at its end which he guessed by the general design of the building gave entrance to the lounge. It did.

He called again, got no answer, and saw the same carpet flowing into the room as he pushed the door standing ajar as the front one had been.

As he entered the room he was facing a wide and high window looking out of the grounds, an almost dazzling green under the sunshine of the morning. When his eyes had adjusted to the brilliant light and he looked round the room he was quite unprepared for what he saw. There were no obvious signs of anything wrong except that one of the deep green brocaded armchairs had been pushed askew and was facing the door, not the Adam style fireplace. The matching settee had also been pushed round so that Garvey's first sight of Larkin was his shoe protruding over the edge of the settee. The solicitor was flat on his back along the cushions staring up at the ceiling. There was blood at his mouth. One hand was hanging down fingers curled. The other was across his middle gripping a Luger-like pistol. Garvey had no need to look twice to know that Larkin was dead. The mess behind his head was indescribably gory though the reporter made no attempt to look closely or to move it. He had always loathed the sight of death. It made him weak. He hurried from the room to find a toilet.

When he got back he was sufficiently

recovered to act precisely. He found a telephone in a small room fitted out as a study and in the best tradition of detective fiction wrapped his handkerchief round the instrument before he lifted it. He dialled 999 and asked for the police. When he got them he asked for Detective Sergeant Grout. There was a faint chance that the CID man would be there, but Garvey knew him and it was well worth telling Grout what had happened rather than go through the laborious details normally asked of a stranger.

Grout was at his desk in the CID room as it happened.

"Jesus H. Christ!" he blasphemed immediately. "Hang about, Tom. We're on our way. Trees Court? No. 10?"

They arrived after seven minutes, the sirens dying to a respectful moan as they entered the grounds of Trees Court. They filed into the bungalow, Detective Chief Inspector Savage, Sergeant Grout, finger-print men, photographers and the police surgeon, one after the other as un-emotionally as visiting plumbers. Garvey had been telephoning meanwhile. He had contacts with the London evening papers and the local one at Portsmouth.

The corpse was left to the mercy of the technical men while Savage with Grout in attendance spoke to Garvey in the study. The newspaper man let it be known that he was seeking Miss Tatchell and produced his copy of the telex to support his action. Nor did he fail to mention his and Beckworth's suspicions that an attempt was being made to steal the lady's inheritance. Both Savage and Grout looked suitably solemn on hearing this but did nothing about it other than to tell Garvey to wait where he was and not to leave till he was given permission. Garvey got back to telephoning. He could see the headlines already. "*Globe* reporter finds prominent solicitor dead."

The police continued their work with their customary infinite patience. Neighbours were questioned but apart from their shocked reaction to the news had nothing noteworthy to offer by way of evidence. Nobody had heard the shot or shots but this surprised no one. As far as could be ascertained Charles Larkin had left for work driving his grey Granada at his usual time of nine twenty. After about an hour he had come back again. This was not unusual and the car was in the garage. The witness who had seen it return was not prepared to swear that Larkin had been driving it or that he had been alone. He *thought* he had seen another car drive in the main entrance shortly afterwards but which bungalow it had visited he didn't know, nor had he seen it leave. Colour? Might have been blue. Make? They all look alike to me.

The team within the bungalow were having better results. A meticulous examination of the lounge had revealed a bullet hole almost exactly in the angle where the wall joined the ceiling and not easily discernible.

"Cripes!" Grout exclaimed in his loud voice, "don't tell me he missed himself with his first shot!" Up till then they had been taking it for granted that it had been suicide. Then the police surgeon, who was an irascible gentleman with an untidy shock of grey hair and deep set eyes that looked perpetually angry, added to their doubts by snapping:

"Not my business to point this out. Up to the pathologist when he deigns to get here. But the bullet smashed the front teeth. Means the mouth was closed when the gun was fired. Not exactly typical of a suicide."

It was nearly lunchtime before Garvey was told that he was no longer required. He had lost some patience by then. He tapped the copy of the telex.

"What are you going to do about this, man?" he demanded of Sergeant Grout. "Three and a half million dollars worth of bearer bonds. I told you earlier. Don't you think you should check with the bank what's happened to 'em? Larkin may have blown his brains out or somebody may have done it for him but these damned bonds are behind it." He went on to tell him about Deacon, the ex-convict whom Larkin was employing as a managing clerk and Grout finally referred it to Chief

Inspector Savage, who had just given himself the unenviable task of finding old George Larkin so that he could tell him of the death of his son.

Savage asked more questions.

"Southern County Bank, eh? Better get round there," he told Grout. "I know the manager, Mr. Sharp. I'll speak to him on the blower. This is no time for him to get on his high horse."

Grout had no objections to Garvey accompanying him to the bank, but they were shown into a waiting room on arrival to wait Mr. Sharp's pleasure, which didn't please the sergeant at all.

"Ain't it marvellous?" he bleated in his honking voice. "Here we are investigating a possible murder and we have to wait the pleasure of some tin-pot little bank manager, sitting here like a couple of kids expecting to get their backsides tanned. If he comes out with that crap about getting a magistrate's warrant before he'll give us any information I'll croak the little bastard myself! I swear I will. You don't

170

even need a warrant to arrest a guy for murder but to get a bloody bank . . ."

Sergeant Grout's tirade was interrupted by Mr. Sharp himself who hurried into the room almost breathlessly. Garvey wondered how Grout had guessed him to be a little man for that was what he was. His name belied his appearance. He was plump and bald with baby blue eyes and a pink complexion as if he were straight out of the barber's chair.

"I know why you are here," he said briskly. "I've just been speaking to Chief Inspector Savage. He said something about a telex."

Garvey produced it yet again now somewhat bedraggled and Mr. Sharp smoothed it out with chubby fingers before reading it.

"Extraordinary," he declared. "The Americans appear to have no real regard for the confidentiality of a client's business. The bonds arrived here yesterday."

"But have they been taken out again?" Grout demanded.

The bank manager tightened his pursy little mouth and nodded. He looked mournful.

"This morning soon after we opened. It was preposterous!" he burst out. "My staff had not even had time to enter the numbers in the bond register. I told Miss Tatchell as much."

"If it was Miss Tatchell, which of course it was not," Garvey put in blandly. "You'd never met the lady before she came in and asked you to get her account transferred from Carrs, had you?"

Mr. Sharp was not slow in seeing the implications behind what had happened. He stared at his visitors aghast.

"But . . . but Carrs acted upon the transfer order. She signed it here in my room in front of me. And this morning when she withdrew the bonds they were going to her solicitor's office. I insisted upon one of my staff acting as escort. Really . . . I . . ."

Mr. Sharp lapsed into a baffled silence his eyes as hurt as a whipped puppy's.

Garvey glanced at his watch and drew Grout's attention to it.

"One o'clock," he observed. "She's due out of Heathrow at three. Better get a move on, man."

10

BECKWORTH found it difficult to believe that he had actually found Miss Tatchell. He moved along the fence stopping every few yards to bring the glasses up to his eyes in an effort to get a better view of her. When he thought he had reached a point where the distance was the shortest between himself and the reclining figure he shouted her name at the top of his voice and waved. She took no notice whatsoever. He realized that she could not have heard him and, of course, if she were without her contact lenses she certainly could not see him.

The sergeant put two fingers to his mouth, and after several attempts succeeded in letting out a piercing whistle. This, he thought, had been heard. She lifted her head but obviously could not see him. He was reluctant to keep up the noise. It had already sent the moorhens and the coots scurrying across the water. If by any chance the Clints kept some sort of surveillance going, though it was difficult to see how this could be done, then the disturbed birds might have been noticed even if nothing had been heard.

Tatch without either lenses or glasses was as good as blind and no amount of whistling or shouting was going to be of use. He would have to get out to the island somehow. He recalled the gates. The stout chain and padlock securing them would need bolt cutters to cut them. He doubted if the railings of the fence itself would yield to any sort of tool except an oxy-acetylene torch. He was sure he would never be able to steal the one in the Clint's yard and get it down to the lakeside without being detected. Nor did he think he would be able to get away with filching the Clints' boat to get to the island if he succeeded in breaking open the gates. He had no tools in his car except the handle of the jack and he doubted if it was strong enough to use as a lever. Could he get over the fence?

He walked round its western end soon losing sight of Miss Tatchell whose chair was facing south. He recalled that the bank of the lake had looked as if it was bordered by a wood at this point. He reached it to find that the possibility of an intruder using a tree to get over the fence had been foreseen and a wide swathe had been cut through the copse. However, the timber cut down had not been removed entirely but had been piled in an untidy heap at the edge of the copse. Beckworth wondered if he had the strength to move one of the smaller trunks back to the fence, lift it, and then allow its thinner or topmost end to drop over the top. The smaller branches still attached should enable him to jam the tree there tightly enough for him to climb it and to lower himself over the other side. He would still have to get out to the island having accomplished this. Without a boat he would have to strip down to his underpants and swim. Nothing to that, he thought. His build of wide shoulders and plenty of bulk had made him an easy swimmer though it had been years since he had done much of it.

He began heaving the felled timber to one side trying to find a trunk that would suit his purpose. The trees, mostly birch, had been there some time and their branches had mingled with the result that they seemed to be clinging to each other with a fiendish obstinacy that had him sweating before long. He found a length of railing that for some reason had been cut out of the fence during construction. Using it as a lever he was able to free a fir from the pile which he thought would make him a ladder. It was long enough and not too back breakingly heavy. He had yet to drag it as far as the fence. It proved to be hellishly hard work. The smaller branches caught in the earth. It was like a beast digging in its heels reluctant to be led.

He was half way to the fence when the shot came. The almighty thud of the bullet ploughing into the earth close to his feet and the crack of the rifle reached him simultaneously.

Beckworth let the tree drop. A man some hundred and fifty yards distant was standing close to the fence on its outside. He had a rifle in one hand. With the other he made signs indicating that Beckworth should clear off. He shouted as much though the sergeant could not hear him. The man was dressed in black overalls and was bearded; this was all Beckworth could make of him at the distance, but unless he was much mistaken it was the same fellow he had seen at work with the oxy-acetylene torch earlier. One of the Clints?

The sergeant moved, and quickly. There was plenty of cover to hand and he could be behind it almost before the man had the rifle to his shoulder again, and certainly before he could get any sort of aim on a moving target. As he reached the trees another bullet smacked into a trunk nearby. The rifle, Beckworth thought, was at least a .303 and from the brief glimpse he had been given of it from a distance it was an old short Lee Enfield. And a damned efficient weapon at that. He had nothing.

The thought made him snatch up the piece of railing about a yard in length which he had been using as a lever. The wood had little depth and few trees of any real size but Beckworth reaching an oak with a trunk of some girth came to a halt and put the tree between himself and the gunman, who was advancing steadily towards the wood.

Jeff Clint had little tactical sense and was not bothered to use it because he considered Beckworth to be a chance intruder whom his shots had succeeded in frightening away. He fully expected to see him running across the open ground beyond the copse and had no intention of making any oblique move in order to cut him off. He had not recognized Beckworth as the man he and his twin brother had been paid to beat up in his garden three months previously.

He came through the copse and when he reached the oak tree hiding

Beckworth, Clint could see the wide open spaces of the old parkland beyond. He was grinning with the thought of the scare he had put into the intruder with his first unheralded bullet. Failing to see his quarry ahead gave him a sudden feeling of apprehension and he came to a halt. He heard the whistle of Beckworth's piece of rail as it came through the air towards his head. He dodged the worst of it but it caught the side of his ear with such pain it bemused him. The next blow felled him as if he had been hit with a seven-pound sledge. He dropped flat and lay still with his skull cracked and his torn ear streaming blood.

Beckworth discarded his railing and picked up the rifle. As he had thought it was an old short Lee Enfield and it had a V backsight. He knew something of guns and appreciated the fact that the man he had knocked unconscious must have aimed to miss, at any rate with his first shot. With this supremely successful rifle old as it was he could, after taking deliberate aim, have burst a rook apart at a hundred paces never mind hitting an object as wide as a man.

Beckworth thumbed on the safety. With one hand he groped round the unconscious man's body for his wallet while with the other he kept a grip on the rifle. After all there were supposed to be two Clints and the other, equally hostile, might not be far away.

He found a bulge in a hip pocket . . . the sucker pocket Beckworth considered it . . . and took out a wallet. Identification was obtained from a grimy looking driving licence in the name of Jefferson Clint; a posh sounding name he thought for this scruffy number, who with his brother had been employed to beat him up. Beckworth could sniff him. It was not a farmyard odour about him as he had once thought but one from the scrapyard; a mixture of acetylene gas, of hot metal and oil.

He was considering his next move when in the distance he heard a man's shout. It sounded like, "Jeff!" Knowing the sound to have come so far away that an answering voice would not be recognized Beckworth bawled back: "Here!" He moved himself till he could see the caller coming along the fence towards him, and then returned to stand over his victim, the rifle at the ready. The second Clint, much closer now, called again but Beckworth made no answer. He waited.

Dag Clint came up to the edge of the copse and there he paused, sensing that all was not well with his brother. He moved forward again cautiously. He was unarmed. It was not the first time the rifle had been fired to frighten off casual but unwanted visitors; week-end picknickers sometimes. Some of them, scared and shocked, had reported it to the police but the Clints were adept liars and of course skilled in hiding the rifle when the police came looking as they had done on occasion.

Beckworth allowed him to come close before he stepped in front of him, rifle poised for a shot that would have taken the man's stomach away.

"That's far enough. Stand right where you are, mister!"

Clint's amazement was comical. Although he had no beard his face was covered with black stubble and he contrived to look as hairy as his brother. He was plainly a twin. The same dark eyes, his as cunning looking as a wary pig's. The same bulbous lips. The same build, shortish but thick set. The only difference was in the colour of his overalls, which were brown, but nearly black from use. His shocked amazement gave way to anger when he saw the condition of his brother.

"Fer Chrissakes!" he snarled. "He was only firing to scare you off. He could've shot your head off yer shoulders if he'd wanted. You've cracked his skull open!"

"So I have," Beckworth agreed amiably. "Ain't that sad? Exactly what was done to mine in my own garden by you two bastards three months ago, or had you forgotten?"

Clint stared at him, apprehension showing in his eyes.

"So?" he demanded. "You'll have a job to prove it."

"Meaning you were dressed up as Mickey Mouses?" Beckworth jeered. "I could identify you and your twin by the smell of you. You stink of that scrapyard. Empty your pockets. If you've got a gun in one of 'em don't try to use it or I'll blow off your kneecap."

Clint was still defiant.

"Yeah? You're bluffing, Dad. You wouldn't dare use that rifle. You wound me and you're in real trouble."

Beckworth laughed.

"Listen, you ignorant scum. I'm a cop. I've been thirty years a cop. D'you think I don't know the drill? How many times have I heard the beak ask, 'How did the prisoner come by his injuries?' and how many times have I heard the reply, 'He fell down the stairs to the cells, your worship.' Be your age, Clint. This time it will be, 'He had a rifle, sir. Exhibit A. I grappled with him and it went off, the bullet striking him in the kneecap, sir.' Whose story is going to be believed,

184

Clint? Yours with your form? Or mine because I'm a cop? When I get you to court you're going to be condemned before your brief has had time to open his mouth. Empty your pockets."

Clint obeyed the order. When he had finished Beckworth still with the rifle ready for instant use patted him all over for a concealed weapon using his free hand.

The small heap of pocket contents contained a note case, small change, cigarettes and lighter, a filthy handkerchief, and two lots of keys on rings. One of these held only two keys, one of them short but fat looking as if it might be the key to the heavy padlock on the gates in the fence and the other, somewhat smaller, could also have been a padlock key. Beckworth helped himself to these, looping their ring on one finger.

"Okay," he said. "Pick it all up again. I'll have these." He dangled the two padlock keys. "It's my guess one of 'em opens the padlock on the gates in the fence. Right?"

"Right."

Clint had been digesting the information, not without sweating, that his captor was a cop. This had been entirely beyond his reckoning. His past experiences at trials from which he had managed to wriggle away free until the last when he had been convicted, his long prison sentence, and until recently the close eye that had been kept upon him after release, all had made him hate policemen deep in his guts. But he also feared them. The idea that he and his brother had actually beaten this one senseless not knowing he was a cop frightened Clint nearly witless. He saw now that Beckworth was most obviously a cop; an ageing one maybe but a policeman. And now he was one with a score to settle. Jesus! The bastard could kill him and probably get away with it.

"Listen, mister," he pleaded desperately, "we didn't know. We weren't told you were a cop. I swear to God we wouldn't have laid a finger on you . . ."

"Bull," Beckworth snorted. "Who

186

hired you? Deacon, or Bishop to give him his real name, is my guess."

Clint nodded.

"Where d'you meet him? In stir?"

Again the nod.

"How much did he pay you?"

"A monkey each."

"I'm flattered, or did that include payment for snatching Miss Tatchell . . . the woman you're keeping on the island?"

"We didn't do the snatch, mister. We just . . ." Clint's voice died away as his brother groaned loudly. He failed to stir, however, but his breathing became suddenly stertorous.

"We'll talk about Miss Tatchell later," Beckworth said. He nodded at the man on the ground. "He's Jefferson. What's your handle?"

"Dagworth."

"*Dagworth?*" Beckworth hooted in derision. "My God! Your folks liked fancy names. Pick him up!"

"Jeeze! By myself? I don't know if I can manage . . ."

"Pick him up," Beckworth repeated

coldly. "That is if you want him to have medical aid. If not, leave him. But you'll be with him minus a kneecap. I can't be lumbered with you two bastards. I've other things to do before I phone for an ambulance. Do as I say. Pick him up!"

For all his protest suggesting that he might need help and prompted by the idea that he might trick Beckworth while his brother was being manhandled between them, Clint managed to get the unconscious man across his shoulders in a fireman's lift.

With Beckworth following he started back towards the eastern end of the lake.

11

TRAILING behind Dagworth Clint's loaded figure, which lurched at times over the uneven ground, the sergeant considered what he should do next. He needed to take Miss Tatchell off the island and safely back to her home. That must be his prime objective. However, he had two bad men on his hands and he was not disposed to let them off lightly due to the circumstances. One of them was seriously hurt and whilst Beckworth had about as much regard for the injured Clint as he would have had for a wounded stoat, which he would have put out of its misery anyway, he had to comply with the rules of civilized behaviour.

The Clints had brought the boat on its trailer as far as the outside of the fence close to the gates. It was their practice to make a cursory survey of the lake's surrounds before venturing out to the island, or even opening the gates, because they were not supposed to use the lake let alone have a key to the padlock securing it. This had been achieved by cutting away the original official one and substituting one of their own. They wanted no casual witnesses to their periodic visits to the island. Thus they had caught sight of Beckworth struggling with his reluctant fir towards the fence.

By the time Dagworth Clint had deposited his unconscious brother in the back of their old car he was well nigh exhausted, and Beckworth had made up his mind what to do. Tatch had been on the island for three months or more by now and another few minutes there while he attended to more pressing if relatively unimportant matters were not going to harm her.

"We'll take this sleeping beauty back to the house," he told Clint. "You can phone for an ambulance. Who lives in the house besides you two?"

"Only the old woman, our Ma."

"No wives?"

"Naw. I'm a bachelor. His wife left him when he was inside."

Beckworth was aware that the active Clint was eyeing him with all the malignity of an angry boar. He hefted the rifle.

"OK," he nodded. "Unhitch the trailer. And get this straight, Dagworth, you venomous object. Don't try any tricks while we're on our way or as sure as God made little apples I'll let you have it. Just remember that on the move my aim might be less accurate. I could hit you in a vital part. Too bad. Get moving."

The boat was made of fibre glass and easily handled on its trailer which Clint unhitched and pushed towards the gates where he left it. The boat was empty and a thought came to Beckworth when he observed nothing but the motor on its stern.

"Why were you going out to the island?" he demanded. "I mean . . . I know damned well you're keeping Miss Tatchell a prisoner there. I came looking for her. But why the visit . . . now?

You've no supplies aboard. Nothing. I thought you'd learnt of my presence down by the lake somehow and came to investigate. But that ain't so. You took the trouble to hitch on the boat, which you wouldn't have done if you'd just come looking. So?"

Clint hesitated. The answer needed careful thought. He knew Deacon to be on his way and whilst the solicitor's clerk had no love for the Clints, or they for him, he would at least side with them against this cop. But he must answer convincingly.

"I think," Beckworth declared, "that it has something to do with your being absent when I arrived. Only this bird, working in the yard, was to be seen. What's on, Clint? Don't keep me waiting. Where were you?"

"In Chichester."

"And what were you doing there that made you decide as soon as you were back to go out to the island? Come on, you bastard! Answer me. I swear to God I'll . . ."

"Fer Chrissakes!" Clint yelled, "I was after our money. We've been promised payment for days. Bishop . . . Deacon said he'd be out with it later today or first thing tomorrow."

"And you believed him?"

Clint spat expressively.

"Why not? He knows we'll blow the gaff on 'im this time for sure if he don't turn up. Listen, mister, you know what he's been up to, don't you? 'E snatched that dame on the island and brought 'er here so that 'is missus could take her place and collect the money she's inherited from the States. Well, it's arrived. The Yanks sent it off five days ago . . ."

"I see," Beckworth nodded. "I get the picture. So now the evidence has to be disposed of. I've arrived like the hero in a serial film, ain't I, Clint? In the nick of time. You were on your way to the island to slit the lady's throat, or maybe drown her in the lake, weren't you?"

"No. No. You got it wrong, mister. We don't hold with murder. But that's what

Deacon will do." Clint found voice with a gush of words. "We was aiming to take her off the island to a relative of ours the other side of Farnham for a couple of days then let her go. Why should we want to kill 'er? She ain't a bad old bird. And she's nearly blind, anyway. You could stand a bloody great 'orse in front of her and she wouldn't see it. She could never get up in court and identify us, could she?"

Beckworth had considered the matter of identification before then. The idea that the Clints might escape their just dues because Tatch could never have actually seen them was an unsavoury one yet true. But the same could not apply to Deacon, however, whose best interests would be served if she went to the bottom of the lake. At the same time he could not think that the Clints' motive in moving the lady was at all altruistic.

The sergeant nodded.

"So you don't hold with murder, Clint? I wish I could believe you. I really do. You're so convincing. I can almost see the halo round your stinking head. I expect the real reason is that knowing Deacon is on his way with the pay out you decided to move her off the island and put up the ante."

Beckworth's disbelief in the Clints' motive for moving Tatch, if that had been their intention at all, had blinded him to the fact that Dagworth might also have lied about the time of Deacon's expected arrival. It certainly never occurred to him that it might be imminent.

"I ought to shoot you, and leave you to rot alongside your brother," he snarled. "Get in the car. You're driving us up to the house. I'm not allowed a private vengeance, Clint, but . . . no tricks, or I might forget it."

Within five minutes they were outside the house. Clint manhandled his brother into the kitchen. Beckworth following him heard the old woman's shrill questions.

"Don't argue, Ma," Clint snarled at her. "Get on the blower and dial 999 for an ambulance. Tell 'em there's a cop here already if they want to know."

"Police! Them pigs . . ." The old woman let out a flow of invective aimed at the police in general and Beckworth in particular. She spat at him as she saw him loom up in the doorway rifle at the ready. Then she went into the hall to telephone.

Beckworth never waited to hear the result. If she hadn't the sense to get medical aid to her son that was no concern of his. Clint had deposited his brother's inert but loudly breathing form into an old rocking chair the old lady used for leisure moments. It stood in front of an Aga cooker.

"Right!" the sergeant snapped. "You can't do any more. Back to the lake!"

The ancient Zephyr rattled through the yard and over the grass hill behind it swaying and bumping as if it was about to fall apart. Beckworth clung on sure that Clint was driving erratically by choice hoping the movement might throw him out. It didn't.

Beckworth flung him the key to the gates on its ring.

"What's the smaller key for?" he asked idly.

Clint was strangely hesitant.

"I asked you a question, Clint."

Still there was no answer and the sergeant, losing patience, swung the muzzle of the rifle at the side of Clint's head. He saw it coming and dodged the worst of it but it hurt. He rubbed the spot, murder in his eyes.

He nodded towards the island.

"She's wearing an iron belt . . . sort of corset with lead weights in it . . . locked round 'er by a padlock. That's the key. So she can't swim for it, mister. She'd sink carrying that weight."

"And she's been wearing it since she's been there?" There was an amazed sort of awe in Beckworth's voice.

Again Clint's nod. The sergeant swore.

"Jesus God!" he breathed. "Not content with robbing her of her contact lenses and glasses so that if she did attempt to swim for it she'd probably go

197

round in circles, not to mention this damned great fence she'd have to get over, you bastards have to make sure she doesn't even try it."

"It was Deacon's idea, guv'nor. Straight up. We ain't hurt her."

"No? God help you if I learn differently, Clint. I'll see you wear the iron belt, then I'll kick you into the water and watch you drown."

Clint was oddly defiant on this point.

"I said we ain't hurt her and I meant it. We don't fight women, mister, or knock 'em about. It's that Deacon you want to watch. He ain't the big pansy he pretends to be. You know what he's got planned for her? This lake is full of eels. It's the warm water attracts 'em. He'll tip her in. 'The eels will eat her,' he says and enjoys the thought."

Clint was warming towards the conversation. He was playing for time expecting the arrival of Deacon at any minute and subsequent rescue for himself from the attentions of this menacing old cop. Beckworth wondered, if it was true about the

198

eels, why Miss Tatchell's body had not been fed to them months previously. Clint started off again but the sergeant cut him short.

"Get those gates open, and the boat into the water. You'll follow me into it when I say so. You'll drive. Don't forget I can fire this rifle more quickly than you can tip me into the water. I'll have the keys."

Clint did as he was told. He tried to waste more time while he tugged uselessly at the toggle to start the motor. But he had enough sense to realize that if he overdid it Beckworth would guess his intention and the reason for it. He gave the motor the required throttle setting and it sang into life.

The journey to the island took barely three minutes. Clint steered the craft to the usual landing spot on the north bank which had been revetted with rows of wooden stakes to form a makeshift quay. Beckworth had to make up his mind who was to alight first. He knew that he could not trust Clint for a second, but the island was heavily wooded and if Clint was first ashore he might take a chance and dodge quickly out of sight. Beckworth had no idea what was on the island but it was possible that Clint might know of something to hand with which he could threaten the defenceless Tatch's life unless the rifle was dropped. The sergeant decided to get out of the boat first, which he contrived to do fairly easily without taking his eyes off Clint.

But he had failed to consider that Miss Tatchell, though near blind, had nothing wrong with her hearing. Ordinarily when she heard the boat's outboard buzzing towards the island she knew that it was the Clints with supplies, but they invariably came in the late evening in the last of the daylight in order to avoid chance witnesses. This mid-morning visit had her puzzled. The island had only two paths that could be called such across its breadth, one from the landing to the hut and the other to the south bank where she sun bathed. She knew her way along these if she moved carefully. Her sight could distinguish objects in front of her but not the nature of them. She had heard the boat's approach and was on the path, a yard or two from the quay as the sergeant got out not seeing her because of his watch on Clint.

She called:

"Who is it?"

Beckworth, without thinking, replied immediately.

"It's me. Len Beckworth. Come to take you home, Tatch."

It was for him a moment of triumph. He had found her in spite of his often held conviction that he never would, at least not alive. Not only that, if Clint were to be believed, he had found her just in time and it was small wonder that he wanted her to know that she was free the moment he saw her. But he had not reckoned on her reaction.

For a few stupefied seconds she stood still saying nothing then she cried joyfully:

"*Len!* You old bastard! You've found me. Oh, God! I *knew* you would. I *knew* it." She rushed towards him. "Where the hell are you? I can't see you properly."

She blundered into him, wrapped her arms round him, found his face and kissed him, unaware that he had a prisoner he needed to watch and a rifle he might have to use, and that she was making it impossible for him to do either.

It was enough for Clint. He had let the motor die prior to securing the boat by its painter to one of the stakes. Now he scrambled back to the stern, heaved the motor to life again by its toggle, and while Beckworth struggled out of Tatch's embrace, he opened the throttle.

The boat surged away in a triumph of sound curving out of sight round the island before the sergeant could find an aim.

12

ARTHUR BISHOP, alias Deacon, drove carefully along the Petersfield road towards Harting and the Clint brothers' scrapyard. This in his estimation was the start of the final lap and he wanted no silly slip up such as a last moment road accident to ruin it. Not only that he had just met up with and overcome a totally unexpected obstacle which if it had not left him nerveless had come very close to it. For a time he had felt shaky, but it was wearing off and before he reached the Clints he would be himself again. And he would need to be because the Clints would be troublesome. He had no intention of paying them the huge sum, ten per cent of the inheritance, they had been demanding for looking after Miss Tatchell.

Charles Larkin had been responsible for the Clints. It was he who had insisted upon no harm coming to Miss Tatchell, and he had been far too free with the information he had given them in staving off their incessant demands for payment on account. But, of course, they had been a menace. Which was why he was on his way to make a final reckoning with them; keeping a deadline he dared not ignore. Deacon's thoughts were grim enough to make the huge hands clamp the steering wheel and his teeth to show in a mirthless grin. He had killed once. One or two more were not going to matter. The Clints would go the same way as the woman, into the lake. Food for the eels. Give the slimy creatures something to eat.

His mind turned to the past. Getting a job with Larkin, Brown and Larkin had been an economic necessity and nothing more at the time. It had been typical of Charles Larkin not to have followed up the faked references though they had been works of art, which might have excused him.

But a clerk's salary had never been Arthur Bishop's idea of a permanent reward for his services, and he had kept an eye open for anything that might lead to better things. The death of Octavius Brown, and the strange reluctance of Charles Larkin to take on another partner, had set Deacon, always prying for the main chance, wondering why. Before that Larkin had become mixed up with an actress and his wife had divorced him. The actress, Deacon had been told, had been followed by other women equally expensive. Was it possible that Larkin had been helping himself to a client's money?

Deacon himself, as Arthur Bishop, had been expert enough in that though he had finally been caught. He didn't think it was the Clients' Account. The auditors were always too careful checking that but Larkin handled the trusts. Had he been at one of those? It had taken a long time to pin-point it. Ten thousand pounds worth of Government stocks had been sold off the Wilson Trust on Charles Larkin's order and not reinvested.

Deacon had done nothing, said

nothing, at the time. It was just a little piece of comforting knowledge warm at the back of his mind like an insurance against possible hard times. He soldiered on, his own knowledge of the law a tremendous aid to Larkin still without another partner.

When the odd enquiry about Miss Tasmin Tatchell from Green, Schultz and Parmenter, Attorneys-at-Law, in Dallas, Texas, had reached them Deacon had at once seen the possibilities behind it. A similar letter had been sent to all solicitors in the area because old Beamish had known only that his family had originated there, and when Deacon had learnt this it seemed obvious to him that the old gentleman must have a fortune to leave although he was described as a chicken farmer, which description had been passed on to Miss Tatchell but nothing more; certainly not the idea that her old uncle had riches to leave.

Deacon had thought it worth-while to engage the services of a Dallas firm of private enquiry agents to delve into the history of Thomas Ralph Beamish. Their report had been a fulsome one including the details of the sale of his land to Consolidated Oil Products in return for five million dollars in COP bonds, and bearer bonds at that. Unfortunately the Dallas enquiry agents' bill had been a heavy one which Deacon had been quite unable to meet. That was when Larkin had been drawn into the plot.

Deacon could well remember it. Using his customary obsequious pose he had gone into the partner's office one morning, smirking with humility as usual though he hated Larkin's guts and always had done.

"I wonder if you will kindly sanction payment of this bill, Mr. Larkin, sir? From America. They are private enquiry agents. Here is their report."

Larkin had read both, his veined eyes bulging when he had seen the amount of the bill.

"Two thousand five hundred dollars! What the hell is this? Who asked you to employ these people?"

"Oh, nobody, sir. I took it upon myself. I'm sure you will see the wisdom of it, sir. Miss Tatchell knows nothing about it. Five million dollars, Mr. Larkin, sir. And in bearer bonds at that. It has tremendous possibilities for you and me, Mr. Larkin, sir. Why, you'll be able to replace the Government Stocks you sold off the Wilson Trust, won't you? And take a little more besides, of course."

For a moment he had thought that Larkin, comparatively young man though he was, would have a stroke. The solicitor had stared at him with his cod-like eyes bulging alarmingly while the colour had drained from his face leaving the freckles showing like bread crumbs.

"All right, Deacon," he had said resignedly. "How much do you want?"

"Oh, nothing really, Mr. Larkin, sir. Your secret is quite safe with me. Absolutely. I'll think up a plan for use when Miss Tatchell inherits and let you know. In the meantime if you will just sanction the payment of this bill, sir?"

Deacon could see that one of the

biggest obstacles to be overcome in robbing the inheritance would be the publicity attached to it. He and Larkin could make sure that as far as they were concerned there would be none whatsoever, but the Americans would not be inhibited. The publicity would start there and spread to the English papers.

He had never actually met Miss Tatchell but he made it his business to get a good sight of her. When he realized that in build and general appearance she was not unlike his wife, Philippa, though somewhat older, then the germ of an idea was born. Philippa, God bless her, was an adept at copying with a pen. Indeed, that had been how he had first met her as a client when she had been in trouble with the police through forging her employer's signature on a cheque. She had got away with a suspended sentence for which she'd been duly grateful.

Miss Tatchell's file had provided a letter written by hand and a signature for Philippa to copy and to practise on, which she had done with a praiseworthy intentness till she could produce both at will.

Larkin, however, had proved an awkward conspirator to say the least of him; one who threatened at times to upset the whole damned applecart by his squeamishness and general half-hearted approach. Deacon could well remember how he had been compelled to lecture him.

"We take the lot, Mr. Larkin, sir. Not just enough for you to repay the Wilson Trust, with a bonus for you and me. The lot. And then we get out, sir. Or at least I shall, right out of the country, and so will you."

Of course Larkin had agreed in the end and had indeed bought an air ticket to South America, but what the devil had he expected when once he had started milking the Wilson Trust? That had been the beginning of the end for him, and deep down he had known it.

But he had proved adamant about one thing; no harm must come to Miss Tatchell. Before he would be a partner in murder he would throw in his hand, confess to the depredations he had made on the Wilson Trust, and take what was coming to him. And Deacon had sensed that he had meant it. Because Beamish's executors would expect to pay over the balance of the inheritance after taxes had been paid to Miss Tatchell's bankers the plan demanded that she be impersonated by Philippa. That would not prove insuperable to manage because Philippa would be able to produce her signature on demand, but if the real Miss Tatchell were not safely out of the way, under the soil for preference, who in hell was going to keep her prisoner in the meantime?

This had worried Deacon almost to the point of telling Larkin it could not be done until he remembered the Clint brothers, whom he had met in prison. Unsavoury characters, but hadn't one of them told him that they had a small holding in West Sussex, well isolated, that had been turned into a scrapyard? He had gone out there, driving along the very same road he was now on, and as soon as he had learnt that the Clint brothers lived alone looked after by an old mother as deep in sin as they were, he knew he had the answer. The fenced-in lake adjoining, on which at one time some cranky relative of the old landlord baron had built a hut in which to live a hermit's life on the lake's island, had been an unexpected bonus.

All set. He had arranged with the firm of private enquiry agents in Dallas to be informed of Beamish's demise immediately the old man had drawn his last breath. They'd had good warning. First thing on the day when the news would break in the London evening papers they were calling upon Miss Tatchell. Give Larkin his due. He had handled the situation superbly, persuading the woman to pack up and to leave before the television news crews could get there. She had telephoned her neighbours while Philippa had prepared coffee, heavily doping Miss Tatchell's so that they'd been able to get her into the car and away before the first reporters had arrived. Even Philippa, wearing some of the woman's clothes, had been able to leave before the newshounds had besieged the house. Too bad about the dog. Perhaps he should not have killed it, but it had got on their nerves and if it had gone with her to the Clints it would have been a constant hazard. Who could have known that one of the neighbours she had phoned was a nosey retired copper? Still, the Clints had dealt with him and the bastard was still in hospital for his pains. No problem there.

After that it had been a matter of Philippa moving from one hotel to another registering in the name of Miss Tasmin Tatchell, never staying too long at one, and writing letters to Miss Tatchell's acquaintances, carefully worded to suggest that the sudden prospect of great wealth had given her something of a phobia against publicity, and hinting that it was unlikely that she would ever return to Funtingdon. The transfer of the banking account to a bank where Miss Tatchell was not known had been vital, but it had gone off without a hitch. Then all that had been needed was to sit back, wait for probate and the delivery of the bonds.

Larkin had wanted half. This had not been Deacon's idea of a fair share out at all. With his wife involved he had reckoned on a split of seventy-five twenty-five but the solicitor, upon whom he had to rely for the expenses incurred . . . a thousand to the Clints for dealing with the nosey neighbour, not to mention Philippa's hotel bills . . . had been obstinate. Larkin had been compelled to make a further raid on the Wilson Trust to meet them. This, he had said, entitled him to a solid half share. So be it. But as far as Deacon was concerned it sealed the solicitor's fate. He had needed a hand gun with which he intended to stage Larkin's suicide and it had not been too difficult using prison acquaintances to acquire an old Luger, firing 9 mm ammo, of which he had two clips.

The morning of the pay-out had started badly enough with one of the Clints waiting outside the office door when they had arrived, threatening exposure and the release of Miss Tatchell if payment was not made that day. Larkin had given him the story telling him that the bonds were on their way and that the twins' share would be delivered to them by Deacon just as soon as they had been able to count them. Clint had wanted to stay but Larkin had told him bluntly that his presence in the office at the time of the delivery of the bonds would make it damned obvious that he was involved when the police started enquiries later as they were bound to do since he, Larkin, and the Deacons were skipping the country that day. If he had any sense he would go home and wait for Deacon, who in any event had to call upon them to take Miss Tatchell off their hands. Once she had gone the Clints would be absolutely free of involvement because her state of near blindness while she had been with them would keep them anonymous. What they did with their share of the bonds was their business.

Clint had gone off grumbling. No

sooner had he disappeared when to their intense relief Philippa came in escorted by a clerk from the bank carrying the bonds in a large envelope. He had been instructed the bonds would be returned later in the day.

Deacon had told the staff the previous day that he was going off on holiday as soon as he had settled a small business matter that morning. Larkin had pretended an appointment in London which would keep him there till late and had suggested the office be closed for the day, an offer eagerly accepted by the juniors.

The bonds had been split after putting aside the ten per cent for Deacon to take to the Clints, or so Larkin had thought. Or had he?

Deacon had known that Larkin would be leaving for Heathrow shortly after closing down his home at Trees Court. Philippa had gone off to visit her mother prior to driving to the airport, so that Deacon, the office shut down, followed Larkin home after ten minutes.

Perhaps he should have realized that the solicitor, squeamish as he had seemed when it had come to deciding what should be done with Miss Tatchell, was not quite the soft number Deacon had thought him to be. At any rate he had been totally unprepared for what had happened next.

"Come on in!" he heard Larkin's shout after he had rung for admittance. "The front door's open." Then again as he had stepped into the hall. "In here, Deacon!"

It had not even occurred to him that it was odd Larkin should have known it was he, and as he had stepped into the lounge the whole damned room had seemed to spin in front of his eyes for a moment such was his shock. Larkin was there with a gun in his hand aimed unerringly at his middle.

"I was sure you'd be along," the solicitor said, "planning to take the lot. You're way out, Deacon. *I'm* taking it. Hand 'em over. Then you and I will take a short drive in your car to a quarry I know of. You'll drive. Once there I shall kill you with a bullet from this gun. No one will find your body . . . at least for the time I need to get to South America. I may as well be hanged for a sheep as for a lamb; a line of thought you were doubtless following for yourself, eh? The briefcase, Deacon!"

It was dangling in his huge hand. Larkin had sounded calm enough but he was not used to violence or offering it. The strain showed in his popping eyes and the effect on his odd upper lip pulled up to give him a pronounced sneer.

The briefcase came up with lightning speed knocking the gun upwards. It cracked off with a noise in the confines of the room that pained the ears. The next moment Deacon's balled fist had rammed into Larkin's middle paralysing him. He dropped the gun. Another blow caught him on the chin. He fell backwards on to the settee out to the world.

Had anyone heard the shot? Deacon had forced himself to wait watching the grounds behind the bungalow through the french windows his view taking in the immaculate lawns and in the distance the blue shimmer of the swimming pool. Then a quick inspection of the front. Nobody about. Nobody came. Nothing.

The single round fired had made a neat hole exactly in the angle of ceiling and wall not easy to spot, but Deacon thought that he might as well follow his original intention to make it look like suicide. Perhaps the medics would be able to tell that the victim had been unconscious when he had been shot. Vague memories of a medical term used in a court case came to Deacon's mind. The cadaveric spasm, the grip on the gun, would that work? Provided the appearance of suicide added to the delay in looking for him it didn't really matter.

He picked up Larkin's gun in a handkerchief. A Walther P38. Wonder where he got it? Clamped his hand round the butt, forefinger on the trigger, muzzle to the mouth, your own finger on top of his on the trigger, and off she goes. Not so much noise this time.

What a God awful mess! Wipe off anything you touched and out of the house. Leave the front door ajar. Larkin's prints alone were on it. Into the car and . . . Glory be! *The bonds!* He'd forgotten Larkin's packet of bonds!

He had found them in a small room fitted out as a study in a briefcase like his own share. A simple matter to transfer them without leaving prints. But it had shaken him. The reaction had made him grit his teeth and clamp on the wheel, but he was all right now. Ready to deal with the Clints.

Dagworth came out of the house as he pulled into the yard. Deacon could sense that all was not well with him though he was as usual looking as craftily evil as a man could.

"Where's your brother?"

"In bed. Ma's with him now." This was true. The old woman, fearful of all authority and hating it, had failed to phone for an ambulance as Beckworth had instructed and half suspected she would. Clint lied easily on how it had happened.

"He met with an accident. One of the

wrecks slipped out of the crane's hook as it was lifting. Caught him on the side of the head. He'll be all right. Bit of concussion, Ma reckons."

He was not going to tell this big baboon about the cop on the island. Not yet. It could perhaps be turned to his advantage though he was not sure how. Without his brother he felt vulnerable. The two of them could have handled Deacon easily. Alone he was not sure. He eyed the bulging briefcase on the seat beside the bigman.

"Step inside. We'll settle up."

Deacon shook his head.

"I'm sorry, Clint. I don't trust you. When I've dealt with the woman. You may have moved her. Get in the car. We'll drive down to the lake."

He lifted the briefcase standing it on the floor under his legs.

Clint complied. It was not a bad idea to move out of sight and sound of the house, away from chance visitors. He had his knife strapped in its sheath to a thigh.

He could reach it through the pocket slit in his overalls.

Deacon drove through the yard and over the hill behind the lot down to the gates in the fence, which had been left standing open.

Clint was still undecided what to tell Deacon. Obviously he would have to know about the cop whom Clint didn't trust any more than he did Deacon. As they approached the island the cop could pick 'em off in the boat like clay pigeons, or with a careful aim smash in the boat's bows. You couldn't be sure that he would wait for them to land before he showed his hand.

Clint climbed into the stern of the boat ready to handle the motor and the steering. Deacon followed, his great weight squashing the tiny craft right down in the water. He sat facing Clint with the briefcase across his knees.

"Look, mister, there's something I've got to tell you."

He stopped appalled. Deacon's great

hand had gone into the briefcase. It came out holding the Luger.

"Fer Chrissakes!" Clint cried.

Deacon shot him twice in quick succession. The impact slammed Clint backwards over the motor but he failed to go overboard. Deacon leant forward and pulled him out of the way.

13

IT took Beckworth some seconds to disentangle himself from Miss Tatchell's enthusiastic embrace.

"Hang about," he cried desperately. He charged quickly to the bank but Clint was taking the boat round the island on full throttle. He was familiar with the island and knew that if he kept a certain line with the boat he would be back on dry land by the gates in the fence before Beckworth could struggle through the undergrowth to the eastern end of the island where he would be able to draw a bead on him.

The sergeant saw him tie up the boat and charge through the gateway to the car. He could have taken a snap shot at him for the rifle had an effective range of a thousand yards, but he was a moving target and the fence was in the way once he was outside it. Nor did Beckworth know how many rounds were left in the magazine. He checked this, found it to be three, and made his way back to Miss Tatchell. The months on the island seemed to have made little difference to the lady; certainly not to her mode of speech.

"What the bloody hell is going on, Len?" she demanded. "Those bastards pinched my contact lenses and goggles. I can't see a damned thing properly, only vague shapes."

"I know," he explained. "I was holding one of the Clints at gun point. When you grabbed me he saw his chance and got away. No sweat. He may have gone for another gun but I've still got three rounds in this." He patted the rifle. "Come on. Let's go up to the hut. I'll put you in the picture."

Now that he was seeing her clearly and had time to appreciate it he noticed that she was much thinner, though the experience seemed to have done nothing to age her. Her dark hair showed no traces of grey. Even he could see it was what a woman would have described as a mess. Under the bulge of her brown jersey and above the top of her matching slacks he could see the ribbed outlines of the iron corset she was wearing. Her right wrist carried a dirty bandage. For one normally so smart she looked pathetically shabby and neglected.

"What's wrong with your arm?" he asked.

"A burn," she answered casually. "I've been burning myself quite often cooking on the calor stove."

Her sight again, he thought. God! She must have been half crazy with boredom all that time, not even being properly aware of her surroundings. And frightened too, though she would be reluctant to admit it.

They went into the hut and he saw at once that nearly blind or not she kept it spotlessly clean. There was a cot in one corner and this had been made up with sheets and plenty of red blankets. She must have been needing those lately, he thought. The September nights were coming cold. He saw a small kitchen table against one wall. Next to it was a gas stove fed by a pipe from a bright blue container. Farther along nearer to the door was a metal sink. A rack above it contained white plates. Her food, she explained, was stored in a cupboard. Drinking water was brought to the island in big plastic containers with taps. One was standing close by the sink on a wooden frame. She washed outside in a plastic tub using rain water when there was any in the butt or lake water during the drought.

"They've kept me well supplied with food," she admitted, "I'll say that for the Clints. They're a strange pair of rogues, Len. They've respected me. Only damned thing they failed on is that blasted privvy outside. It stank to high heaven before they'd clean it out."

"Yeah? Well I hope you haven't got too fond of the bastards," he said savagely. "They put me into hospital for three months." He told her what had happened including the death of her poodle whose grave had first alerted him to the possibility of crooked work.

"Deacon I can understand," he finished, "but is Larkin in the plot with him?"

She ignored this.

"Sod Larkin," she declared. "*Three months*, Len! You were in hospital for three months? Oh, Christ! When I realized I was being kept prisoner here . . . it was bloody obvious why . . . I thought, 'Len will find me. He's a policeman. He'll guess what's happened and he'll find me.' But then as the time passed and nothing happened, nobody came I thought, 'Oh, God. He's like all the rest. Doesn't really care. She's a rich woman. She can buy her way out. That's what he's thinking.' And all the time you were in hospital because . . . I'm sorry, Len. Oh hell! Let's get off this stinking island. I think I'm . . ."

Quite suddenly she was crying helplessly. It was so unlike what he had expected of her that for a moment he was astounded, then he realized that it was reaction and he put a clumsy arm round her.

"Hi, come on, Tatch! This ain't like you. I'll soon have you home."

He led her to the hut's only chair, where she sat for a while. In doing so he had felt again the ribs of the belt she was wearing.

"I've got the key to that contraption round your middle," he told her. "Took it off Clint. I damn near shot him on the spot when he told me what it was for. Surely to God you haven't been wearing the belt the whole time? I mean . . . how d'you get on for washing . . . that sort of thing?"

"Once a week," she sniffed, "I had a sort of stand up wash all over. They left me the key. Oh, they behaved themselves, stayed outside and expected me to lock the belt on again. They made sure I'd done so before they left." She stood up, crossed her arms, and whipped the jersey over her head. The action left her practically topless except for a tatty old bra and Beckworth's eyes goggled. She had magnificent breasts.

The belt, constructed of iron rods crudely welded together, which suggested that the work had been done in the scrapyard in spite of Clint's assertion that Deacon had been responsible for it, was like an iron cage round her stomach. The top of it was under her breasts and the bottom of it rested on the swell of her hips. It was lined with what looked like felt, and hung all round with pouches of the same material. The belt was hinged at the back and fastened in front by a small padlock through a ratchet which allowed for expansion.

Beckworth unlocked with nervous fingers, unhooked the ratchet and the belt dropped on to the floorboards with a distinct thud.

He picked it up, hefting it in his hand. It was warm from her body.

"Jesus wept!" he exclaimed. "This must weigh half a hundredweight."

The felt pockets hanging between the

vertical ribs from the top rim contained oblong slabs of lead.

Tatch had scrambled back into her jersey.

"I got used to it, Len, though I wouldn't recommend it as a way to slim." She took a few tentative steps. "I feel as if I've got springs in my legs now."

"We have to think about getting off the island," Beckworth said. "Clint may have gone for another weapon, though it's my bet he may have cleared off. He said he was expecting Deacon later. We're not out of the wood yet, Tatch. These bastards have everything to lose." He realized that if she had been brought drugged to the island she had no real knowledge of where it was, or of the Clints' background. He told her. "So," he finished, "my car is parked about half a mile away. Once we're in it we're only a few miles from home. Looks as if it's going to be my time to strip off and to swim ashore for the boat."

"Hell! I can swim for it as well, Len, with you keeping me straight."

He thought about it.

He left her in the hut and made his way through the island's undergrowth to its eastern end where he could see the gates in the fence and the moored boat. There was not a sign of human activity anywhere. The water birds had ventured out again and seemed to be drifting aimlessly on the lake's placid surface. There was not even a breeze. Bird calls and the buzzing of insects were the only sounds. He still had the binoculars slung round his neck and with the help of these he made a close inspection of the whole area adjoining the gates and behind the Clints' property. He saw nothing. The land appeared to be sleeping under the hazy September sunshine.

He returned to the hut.

"It's like this, Tatch. I'm no olympic swimmer doing a hundred metres in under the minute. I reckon it will take me ten minutes to reach the nearest bank of the lake. That will be the western end . . ."

"Let me come with you, Len," she interrupted.

He shook his head.

"I don't think so. I can strip off, come back with the boat and we shall then both be dressed for the journey home. And better able to deal with any interference we may meet," he added. "According to Clint, Deacon is on his way. He's supposed to be here either late today or tomorrow morning, but Clint may have been lying. We have to take the chance."

He paused, wondering whether or not he ought to elaborate on the reason behind Deacon's visit. It was not only to pay off the Clints but to deal with the problem of Miss Tatchell once and for all. She must have thought along those lines and wondered what would ultimately become of her because she had realized quite early on during her enforced stay on the island why she was there. It seemed to him that apart from her short show of emotion, which he had attributed to reaction, she had taken the whole episode lightly as if no real harm could ever have come to her. Maybe the comparatively gentlemanly conduct of the Clints had been responsible. But one thing he was sure of and perhaps it would be a good idea to impress this upon her, she would not get the slightest consideration from Deacon.

"So," he went on, "ten minutes for the swim and another ten to walk round the lake, get the boat started and bring it back here. Might take less. Say twenty minutes to see us ashore and through the fence on the way to the car. I think we should chance it. I know I have the rifle, Tatch, but I've got to be careful how I use it. You see, if we were to wait here and wait for them to come out in the boat to the island I could pick 'em off like bottles on a wall, but if I were to kill one of them I'd be in deep trouble, villains though they may be. I'm supposed to know the law. At close quarters it 'ud be different. I could plead that I was rushed. If Clint is waiting for Deacon to arrive before they come out here anything could happen. They'll be armed. I reckon we should go now."

The rifle had no sling, nor when he looked could he find anything in the hut from which he could improvise one; certainly no rope nor string. The sheets on the bed tore too easily they were so old.

"I put my foot through one the other night," Tatch offered. "I'm afraid the material would drop to bits once you put some strain on it when wet. It won't support a rifle across your back. You'd better leave it with me, Len. One of 'em sees me standing in front of him waving a rifle it'll scare the living daylights out of him."

"It would me," he grinned. Even if she could see the prospect would be alarming enough. He would have liked to have taken the rifle with him. He didn't think that immersion in water would greatly affect its efficiency, but without a sling it was impossible to carry.

He led her through the trees and saplings growing in profusion on the island to its western bank where he settled her in a tiny coppice of closely growing saplings. She would be completely invisible to anybody approaching from the hut until the last moment. He explained the situation.

"This will make the shortest swim for me to the western end of the lake, Tatch. Longer walk round it to the boat but it'll come easier than swimming."

He explained the working of the rifle to her so that she could find the safety catch, the trigger, and the bolt easily by touch. There was a cut out on the magazine as well. He pointed out its function but left it open. He slammed a round into the breech, applied the safety and told her what she must do if she were called upon to fire it. The trigger had two pulls to it, and he explained how this worked. He was pretty sure she failed to understand this entirely but he couldn't see that it mattered overmuch. If she had to fire the rifle, which God forbid, her sight was such that she was not going to hit anything except by accident. But, Beckworth thought, she would be intimidating enough.

"OK," he said. "Now listen, Tatch. While I'm swimming ashore and getting the boat will be the critical period. That's when we shall be most vulnerable. Clint and Deacon between them could search the island in a matter of minutes, but you will be well hidden here and it will delay them. So *stay here*, Tatch. If they arrive while I'm swimming I shall have heard the boat and *I'll be back*. So when you hear the outboard approaching, and then cut out as the boat reaches the island, do nothing at all, Tatch, even though by the time lapse you're sure it's me. Don't move a finger till you hear my voice. Have you got that?"

"Loud and clear."

She took the rifle, and squatted amongst the saplings with it across her knees, looking, he thought, like a dame in an old-time Western.

He stripped down to his underpants glad that she could not see him properly for he was sure he must cut a ridiculous figure. He left his clothes in a neat pile beside her. After telling her with a reassuring squeeze of her shoulders that he would not be long he trod his way gingerly to the bank and flopped into the water.

His immediate thought was that it was not very warm and that the Electricity Board must have wasted one hell of a lot of money trying to get any worthwhile heat out of it. He swam gently on the breast stroke. He had not gone many yards before he realized that he was not as good in the water as he used to be. The time in hospital must have had a debilitating effect. He had lost weight and bulk, and therefore some natural buoyancy.

The water had a tangy sort of smell of mould and dead vegetation. It seemed heavy. Before long he was gasping for breath. At least, he thought, by the line he was taking for the shore he was invisible from the eastern end where the boat was. The idea that Clint might choose such a moment to return to the island, see him in the water and attack him while he was swimming, filled him with dread. He could visualise the boat's propeller, tiny though it was, slashing into his arms and shoulders. He would never be able to avoid it. He'd be a dead duck all right.

When he reached the bank he stood for a little while half out of the water while his body heaved for breath and he summoned up enough energy for the final haul up on to the bank. He had the choice of taking either the northern or southern route around the lake to the moored boat. He chose the northern. The copse where he had ambushed Jefferson Clint was on that bank and it offered a little cover en route should he need it.

The grassy bank was kind to his bare feet. He jogged along, his breath coming more easily now. He must be cutting a ludicrous figure with what was left of his paunch wobbling ferociously with every step.

Approaching the copse he thought he heard two shots. They were distant but unmistakable; two pinpoint cracks of sound from the eastern end of the lake. Shots all right. Some mallard ducks lifted overhead with a frenzied clap of wings.

Beckworth paused. He could not see the end of the lake as yet. Then he made for the wood at a run. The outboard motor had started up. The boat surged out on to the lake with a sudden buzz of sound.

14

HE had scarcely got his nearly naked bulk behind a shielding tree when the boat's motor cut out again. It was not yet in view so that it had not reached the island whose make-shift landing stage he could see from where he was standing. He was inclined to curse his own stupidity in having left when he could have waited a few more minutes. Common sense told him he could have gone on thinking that way, stayed there all day, and still been caught out. Was the luck changing? Had Clint run out of petrol, or the motor suddenly broken down? If this had happened then he could swim back to the island before Clint could make it because there had been no oars in the boat.

Beckworth moved cautiously till he had a view of the lake towards its eastern end and saw that it was drifting broadside on to him in the middle of the water's stretch. However, he was quite unprepared for the sight of Deacon's huge figure upright in the boat as he moved cautiously towards the stern balancing himself precariously on the way. The prow came out of the water as he reached the stern. Here he stooped, got his hands on something and heaved while the boat rocked. An overalled figure slid over the side into the water with scarcely a splash and disappeared. Beckworth had no doubt that what he had seen had been Clint's body being confined to the deep, and whilst this imparted no sense of loss he was aware that the two shots he had heard had in fact been Deacon putting paid to Clint's account, which meant that the big man was armed.

Beckworth was suddenly horribly distressed and afraid. Perhaps it was because he was unclothed that he felt so vulnerable. Bare feet alone on open ground would have been enough to dismay him never mind the rest of him. He wanted nothing more than to stretch out under the sun and to dry and to rest. The idea that he must start swimming again was utterly repugnant. He doubted if he had the strength to make it back to the island. If he did he would be close to exhaustion, and how then was he going to deal with an armed criminal, who, even if he could be disarmed would still possess in comparison with himself the size and strength of an elephant?

No sooner had he had this thought than others, the result of his training as a policeman, crowded it into the background. Deacon, he was sure, had shot Clint whilst he was in the boat. The motor had started up after the shots, so it must have been Deacon who had taken the boat half way towards the island, and yet he had seen the big man standing up amidships, so to speak, and stepping carefully into the stern. Presumably he had been compelled to leave Clint's body in the stern and had probably taken the boat out leaning across it because there was no room for his own huge carcass next to Clint. Not that it mattered. The point was that Clint could not possibly have told his killer that he, Beckworth, was on the island and armed with a rifle. Deacon would certainly have not have disposed of Clint's body so casually had he thought for a moment that the action was being witnessed. So if he could make it back to the island, Beckworth decided, he would have the advantage of the surprise element. Even Miss Tatchell would constitute that if she jumped up in front of Deacon brandishing the gun.

He heard the outboard start up again and presently the boat glided into the landing stage of the island. He saw Deacon step out holding a briefcase. No sooner had the big man disappeared through the trees than Beckworth made for the water, slipping into it this time as quietly as he could. He had a few more yards to swim by entering the water at the nearest point to the copse where he had been concealing himself, rather than return along the bank to the spot where he had come ashore, but it might save a few seconds of time which could prove important. A longer swim, he thought, meant nothing in his present state. He was going to be utterly exhausted anyway if he got there at all.

The second swim seemed even more of an effort than the first had been. This was because he was unconsciously putting more strength into each sweeping stroke of his arms and frog-like kick of his legs. He could only pray that his heavy breathing would not be heard and that when and if he reached the island he would have enough strength left to heave himself out of the water.

He laboured on allowing the stroke to become slower to conserve his strength. The boat, which Deacon had tied by its painter to the island's bank, was his target. He made it at last. When he reached it he could do nothing for several seconds but cling to the boat's side while his body heaved for breath and his ears rang as his labouring heart pumped the oxygen-seeking blood to his lungs. When the worst was over he moved round the boat to the bank and hauled himself out like a seal and lay there still breathing hard.

When at last he raised his head he could hear nothing of Deacon nor of Miss Tatchell. The island was quiet. Even the birds had stopped their chattering as if the presence of humans had scared them into silence. The insects hummed and the water made little chuckling noises against the boat's hull and that was all.

Then quite suddenly and clearly he heard Deacon's voice from the direction of the island's centre. It was as obsequious as ever.

"Miss Tatchell! Where are you, Miss Tatchell dear? It's Mr. Deacon, Mr. Larkin's clerk, come to take you home. Nothing to be frightened of."

Beckworth thought the man must be standing outside the hut. Obviously he had not yet found Tatch, and she was lying low obeying orders. The sergeant mused on the situation. There had been an edge to Deacon's voice in spite of its usual mealy-mouthed tone. He had probably been calling for a few times while he,

Beckworth, was swimming across, but he had not as yet made any effort to find the lady. Had he been in the hut? If he had, and it seemed likely, then he would have seen the weighted belt Tatch had been wearing, and would be wondering why it had been removed. He could only assume that it had been Clint who had taken it off her. But it would have made him suspicious. Might he not think that she had left the island? That she had been allowed to do so by Clint?

Whilst nothing would have suited Beckworth more at that moment than for Deacon to decide to leave the island because he could not immediately find Miss Tatchell the sergeant was reluctant to think that it would be the last he would see of Deacon if that happened. He had a hatred for villains that was almost pathological. High-born or low-born came the same to him though there was even less excuse for an educated villain than for an unschooled one. He had never had the slightest consideration for one during the whole of his career. No "There, but for the Grace of God, go I" had ever entered the reckoning of Detective Sergeant Beckworth. There was a right and a wrong, and all men except the mentally defective sheltered in institutions should know the difference. It was as simple as that. He hated Deacon and he wanted him destroyed though to get him behind bars was the most he could hope for. But how, for the love of God, was he to accomplish it?

The big man called again. This time he made no real effort to conceal his impatience though his voice was as oily as usual.

"Miss Tatchell! Where are you? I'm coming to find you now. I've given you a chance to show yourself but you won't take it. Come along now. Where are you? I shall find you all right."

Deacon had been into the hut but he had failed to notice the belt lying on the floor. He had expected to see Miss Tatchell, and when it was at once obvious that she was not there he had gone outside again to start calling her.

It occurred to him that the Clints might have removed her from the island though he doubted it. Perhaps she was in the house, but he didn't think that Clint would have asked him inside if she had been. On her own her bad eyesight made her practically helpless. She would have heard the outboard motor of the boat approaching the island as she had done innumerable times before and she would have assumed it to be the Clints, though they had told him that they usually left any visits till the half light of evening. Had this late morning visit worried her and had she concealed herself because she had suspected what he had intended? But how could she have hidden herself in any sort of effective way if she could not see what she was doing?

Deacon began to feel uneasy. Something was wrong. His immediate reaction to sensing the presence of a red light was to get out himself. She was not worth bothering about now he had her fortune, except that she would prove a damning witness. The reason for her non-appearance might constitute a greater danger to himself than failing to find her and to deal with her. He had to know what it was.

He began calling her again, this time taking no trouble to conceal his anger and exasperation. With his precious briefcase in one hand and his gun in the other he began questing round the hut like a shambling bear.

Squatting on the bank by the boat Beckworth heard him calling and blundering around. He hoped that Miss Tatchell would have the common sense to stay where she was and not react in any way to the big man's offers of safety which by now were no longer in keeping with the tone of his voice.

The sergeant gave further thought to his own position. It seemed hopeless. He had nothing on his feet, and whereas the banks of the lake had been grass covered, the barely defined paths across the island were full of sharp twigs and brambles. It was ridiculous, he thought, aiming to immobilize an armed criminal who had the physical characteristics of a Yeti whilst nearly naked himself and with his feet wincing at every step he took. He might have one slim chance, and that was to surprise Deacon, because it was now obvious that Clint had failed to tell the big man of his arrival. He had probably been shot before he'd had the chance. Undoubtedly Deacon intended to do the same to Miss Tatchell once he set eyes upon her. He had to be stopped.

Beckworth wondered if he could find the spot where he had left the island, because Tatch was nearby with the rifle and so were his clothes. He could perhaps circle round the bank in the water without having to swim much. To stay where he was would be courting trouble should Deacon decide to leave the island and come down to the boat. To be seen, perhaps, before he saw Deacon approaching, would be fatal. Ought he to immobilize the boat's motor? Rip off the lead to the plug perhaps? He might need it himself in a hurry and there would be no joy there.

Thinking thus Beckworth slipped into the water feet first. He found that although the island rose steeply out of the water he could find an occasional foothold on the slimy bottom which relieved him of the energy-sapping need to swim. One hand against the rough earth of the bank was a help.

He began moving, half wading, half floating his way round the island taking care to make as little noise as possible. The island's bank looming above his head seemed much the same each time he stopped to try to determine how far he had gone or where he must haul himself out again. Occasional bushes and branches of willow hung out over the water. He had not really memorized the spot where he had left the island because he had not thought for a moment that he would be called upon to return to it. Where the hell was it? Eventually, by lifting himself in the water when he got a foot to hold he started taking his bearings from the lakeside to give him a better idea where he was. He could recall a lone silver birch growing only a few feet away from where he had landed. He saw this clearly. Not far now.

His movement through the water, though by no means noisy, effectively concealed him from hearing what was happening on the island as did the bank high above his head. He paused to listen and thought he heard Deacon's voice again but where precisely the big man was on the island he could not even guess. He must be fairly near, Beckworth reasoned, or he would not have heard him at all with his head below the level of the bank.

He came upon a cluster of willow branches on which the leaves had a yellowish tinge and he thought that these had been on his right when he had flopped into the water. Where the hell was Deacon?

As if in answer to his self-imposed question he heard the big man's voice again, sounding alarmingly near. It was savage now.

"Come on out!" he was bawling. "I'm bound to find you sooner or later, and when I do . . ."

He left the rest unsaid as if he was uncertain which was the more effective; a clearly defined threat or one left to the imagination.

Beckworth thought that if Deacon were to see him clambering out of the water it would be disaster, but get out he must. He would have to chance it.

Using the willow branches for a grip he pulled himself gently and silently out of the water. It meant that he passed through a bed of nettles. They were browned at the edges and drooping from the summer's drought but they stung him along the shoulders and arms with a fiery abundance just the same. Beckworth swore mightily to himself. All this skulking stuff was utterly alien to him and it was making him angry. He thought he heard movement ahead though he could see nothing for the trees and bushes

254

growing in profusion on the island. However, he thought he could see the cluster of saplings where he had left Miss Tatchell. In a few seconds then, by the Grace of God, he would make contact with her and what was more important have his hand on the comforting butt of the rifle.

He moved forward gently, which was not difficult because his feet winced at every step from contact with the rough ground, thick with undergrowth and brambles.

"Tatch!" he called softly. "It's OK. It's me, Len. Stay where you are. I'll be with you in a moment."

Deacon might have heard him but that could not be helped. Tatch by this time must be squatting there, having heard everything and seen nothing, her nerves near breaking point. If he had given her no warning she might have blasted off with the rifle.

He took the last few steps which should have brought her in sight but there was no sign of her, nor of the rifle, nor his clothes. He had obviously picked the wrong spot. Behind him he heard Deacon calling again.

15

DEACON'S voice had now lost all pretence of reason and certainly of humility.

"Come on out, you bitch! I know you're on this island. I'm going to . . ." There followed obscenities which even the hardened Beckworth wondered at. Delivered in the big man's usual mincing tones distorted by rage they sounded unspeakably venomous. Deacon had decided for no real reason except pure chance to explore the eastern end of the island first once he had moved away from the hut, and this had given Beckworth time to go round the island and to get ashore. But his failure to find the spot where he had left Miss Tatchell made him almost as angry with himself as Deacon was with the lady for not coming out of hiding.

The whole situation in the sergeant's

opinion was too stupid for words. He was a city man. The only jungle he had experienced was one of the pavements, not that of the country particularly on this wild island where one bunch of saplings looked precisely like another to inexpert eyes. His shoulders, arms and chest were aflame with tiny red blisters where the nettles had stroked him and this was not improving his temper. He was tired as well after his swimming efforts, affected by a lassitude that demanded he stretch out in the sun and rest. What in hell was he doing blundering around like an elderly Tarzan after an armed crook himself the size of a mastodon? Miss Tatchell was really nothing to him. He wasn't even being paid to find her or to protect her. How in God's name was he going to find her without calling to her, and thereby revealing his presence to the questing Deacon?

The issue was decided for him because quite suddenly he heard the big man approaching on a line that would bring him directly to the spot where he was standing.

Deacon was rapidly reaching the point where he would give up. He was convinced, however, that Miss Tatchell was on the island. He could not understand why she had hidden herself away. She could not possibly have known that it had been he approaching the island in the boat. She must have assumed it to have been the Clints, and had decided on a whim to be rebellious and uncooperative. Deacon could think of no other reason, and the longer he searched for her the more convinced he became that his reasoning was correct. It had not occurred to him for a moment that a third party in the shape of ex-Detective Sergeant Beckworth was on the island. If he had given any thought to Miss Tatchell's neighbour at all it was that the nosey so-and-so was safely in hospital.

The sergeant caught a glimpse of Deacon's light grey suiting as the big man came towards him concealed for the most part by the dense growth of saplings.

Beckworth crouched waiting. Then he saw the man's arm thrust out in front of him holding the Luger looking small in his huge fist. That was the arm he would go for. If he had not lost his old skill in putting a lock on an arm which would break if the owner resisted then Deacon would drop the gun instantly. Come on, you big bastard, he silently encouraged him. Get close enough.

Then Miss Tatchell took a hand. She was not far away. The sergeant had not been too badly in error when he had hauled himself out of the water, though she had failed to hear him or his soft call of reassurance. But she had heard Deacon's utterances from the very first obsequious one he had made. They had become increasingly menacing, finally revolting her and leaving her in no doubt of what would happen to her if he found her. As he came closer so fear mounted in her mind. She had been waiting patiently, hoping against hope that Beckworth had seen the boat with Deacon in it arrive at the island and that he would return. But she realized his limitations. He was no youngster but a year or two older than herself. The time he had spent in hospital must have weakened him considerably. Now that Deacon was so close fear flooded her mind. Not being able to see she could only imagine what was happening and there had been no sound at all from Beckworth who must have drowned.

Deacon called again. This time he sounded almost on top of her. Fear and revulsion brought her to her feet and the rifle to her shoulder in a clumsy aim in the direction of his voice. She remembered the safety but forgot all about the double pull of the trigger. She yanked at it. The rifle leapt in her hands, the butt slapping into her shoulder like a hammer blow and hurting her. The bullet went high above the trees.

Beckworth, poised to leap at Deacon's gun arm, recognized the sound of the shot instantly for what it was. But the big man was shocked into incredulous immobility and frozen in his tracks. Beckworth took his chance and lunged at the gun arm, got his grip on it and twisted it savagely before Deacon knew what was happening. Beckworth was appalled by the sheer size of the man. The arm felt like a small tree trunk and he was frightened that this alone would prevent him from holding the grip.

"Tatch!" he bawled at the top of his voice. "Over here. Quickly!"

She could only be a yard or two away and would gain direction from the sound of his voice. He kept on shouting.

His grip on Deacon's arm and the savage twisting he gave it hurt the big man, who dropped the Luger into the undergrowth. Surprise had given Beckworth that much success but he could not hold the lock. Deacon shrugged himself and flung the sergeant off him like a stag would a dog, so that Beckworth sprawled on the ground. The Luger had disappeared. In spite of his size and weight and the fact that he was neither slow nor cumbersome in comparison, which gave him a tremendous advantage, Deacon disliked close combat. He had no stomach for it. This made him make the initial mistake of looking for the gun. He stooped to begin with then dropped to his knees feeling with his hands amongst the dense matting of grass, weeds and dead growth into which the Luger had fallen.

Beckworth, who had fully expected the big man to follow up the sort of shrugging swipe that had sent him flying, could hardly believe his eyes. He had learnt unarmed combat in a tough school, and although it had been a long time since he had been called upon to use it in earnest he wasted no time. Flat on his back as he was he brought his bare heels together and in an instant had smacked them together at the side of Deacon's head. The blow knocked the big man sideways and made his head ring. The sergeant was on his feet just as quickly after delivering the blow. He darted forward and his knee came up under Deacon's chin. This time the big man went over backwards. All through this Beckworth, though he was no more aware of it than the abrasions the rough going was causing his bare skin, was shouting for Tatch.

He caught sight of her suddenly pushing her way blindly through the surrounding saplings, the rifle in her hands. She had managed to render it useless for firing in an attempt to reload as Beckworth had instructed her. She had opened the bolt thereby ejecting the spent round, the magazine had fed in the next round but she had not moved the bolt forward again positively enough to lock it. She had opened the bolt again but the jaws of the ejector had not gripped. The magazine had fed up the third and last round and the two had jammed in the chamber.

"Throw it, Tatch! Over here. To me!" Beckworth yelled as soon as he saw her.

Freeing it by some miracle of the surrounding undergrowth she tossed it forward in both hands. It fell short but Beckworth got a grip on it in a moment. He saw the nickel nose of the fresh round sticking up out of the chamber and guessed what had happened.

Deacon, who had bitten his tongue when the sergeant's knee had driven up under his chin, had got to his feet mad with pain and anger. He still had his briefcase. Bulging as it was with the stolen bonds he had been reluctant to part with it from his person and had chosen neither to leave it in the car, nor the hut, nor the boat. He had got to his feet and bellowing with rage he rushed at Beckworth swinging the briefcase at his head. If it had connected it would have knocked the sergeant into the lake. But Beckworth was now master of the situation. He dodged the blow and drove the rifle hard into the man's stomach. The breath went out of Deacon with an audible screech and he dropped to his knees. Calmly, measuring his distance, Beckworth swung the rifle again. This time it caught the big man across the side of his head. Deacon keeled over and the breath began going back into him in long-drawn-out squeals.

Miss Tatchell, who could be said to have witnessed the action though dimly, could see enough to know that the sergeant had triumphed and that Deacon's huge bulk was on the ground.

"Is he out?" she asked practically.

"Pretty well so," Beckworth grinned. "Well done, Tatch. He dropped a pistol just about where you are. Feel around and see if you can find it. I'm going to tie him."

She dropped on her knees. She was expert at finding things by touch and her hands pattered rapidly over the ground in circles around her.

The sergeant was equally expert in tying a man. Deacon's eighteen-inch neck provided a tie with which to bind his wrists behind him. His vast shoes were of the lace up type. Beckworth whipped the laces out of these, tied them together and then bound the big man's ankles. Deacon's breath was still an agonized sucking in of air. The blow he had taken from the swinging rifle had rattled his brains. He had no clear idea of what was happening to him.

Miss Tatchell had found the Luger

meantime which she presented butt first to Beckworth.

"Now what?" she demanded. "The sooner we're off this bloody island, Len, the happier I shall be."

"Me too," he grunted. "I'm going to get dressed first. I've hog tied the bastard. He'll keep, I reckon."

Taking the direction he had seen Tatch coming from he soon found the spot where he had left his clothes. She went with him and stood by while he stripped off his wet underpants. He supposed that she just could not bear the thought of being left alone for a moment now. Not that it mattered. She couldn't see anything, and if she had seen anything she shouldn't have done she would have only laughed, like as not. Thirty years ago, he thought with a grin, it would have frightened her. When he pulled his socks on his feet burned and glowed almost as much as his nettle stings from the cuts and minor abrasions they'd suffered while he had prowled around barefooted.

He led her back to the spot where he

had left Deacon, who was now recovering his wits enough to struggle against the improvized ties that were holding him. The briefcase was alongside him and Beckworth picked this up to inspect the contents; a fat packet of bonds. A quick glance at the numbers showed him that there were over three hundred and fifty of them. Each had a nominal value of ten thousand dollars. The dividends were represented by coupons attached each for five hundred dollars and payable every half-year up to the year 2,000. Some had already been cut off. The bonds were quite impressive looking having been printed on thick heavy-duty security paper in reds and browns with pictures of oil rigs on land and sea together with tankers also on the road and at sea all along the top by way of a heading.

"Your fortune is in here, Tatch," Beckworth told her. But what was the use? She couldn't see them.

Deacon was attempting to get to his feet. The sergeant showed him the Luger.

"If you bust loose, mister, you'll get a bullet quicker than I can blink."

The big man swore at him, and Beckworth's hatred and contempt for all villains, never far from the surface in him, came to the forefront again.

"Shut your mouth, Deacon, or I swear to God I'll let you have it."

Inspiration came to him. The man was a murderer. He had seen him tipping his victim's body into the lake. Supposing the belt they'd improvised to keep Miss Tatchell from swimming off the island would go round the big man? It might. Tatch was no sylph and the belt was on a ratchet.

"By God, Deacon. I've got the answer to what to do with you. I reckon that belt you had made for Miss Tatchell, the weighted one, will go round you. You're going for a swim, Deacon. I'll watch you drown. I guess that'll be good compensation for the three months I spent in hospital on your orders."

He heard Deacon mouth something about not being able to swim as he hurried along to the hut to fetch the belt. But Miss Tatchell went with him and put a hand on his arm as soon as they reached the hut.

"Don't be a bloody fool, Len," she snapped. "You've done enough. Leave the bastard here for the police to collect. If you force him into the water and he drowns you'll only be bringing yourself down to his murdering level. You're better than that. Come on. Let's get off this cursed island. I want to go home, Len."

She was right, of course. Hadn't he told Clint that he was not allowed a private vengeance?

He nodded.

He took her down to the boat. She nursed the loaded briefcase while he steered. Within ten minutes they were in the Cortina and half an hour later were in Funtingdon. It was barely lunch time. He had to fetch his skeleton keys to get into Orchard House. Her instant reaction after putting in some lenses and seeing herself properly in a mirror for the first time in three months was to telephone her hairdresser for an immediate appointment.

"God! I'm a mess," she exclaimed.

Beckworth shrugged. He himself was tired, hungry, needed a bath because he smelt of the lake, and his feet were sore. He attended to this while she prepared an alfresco lunch at the bungalow. When they had eaten and not before he telephoned the police in Chichester. He could not speak either to Sergeant Grout or Chief Detective Inspector Savage, which was not surprising, and had to leave an account of what had been happening at the Clints' holding with an astonished desk sergeant.

He drove the lady into the city and dropped her off as close as he could to the pedestrian precinct that housed her hairdresser. Having then parked the car he went along to Carrs Bank in East Street where he dumped the contents of Deacon's briefcase on Mr. Wooley's desk to the utter consternation of its owner and his deep dismay when he learnt that he had transferred Miss Tatchell's account to the Southern County's branch on the strength of a forged signature.

Tom Garvey, notebook and pencil literally at the ready, was waiting for them when they arrived back at the bungalow. He told them what had happened to Larkin. Mrs. Philippa Deacon had been picked up at the airport, and Deacon himself taken off the island by Savage alerted by radio of the situation.

Beckworth reckoned Garvey had earned his story. For good measure he and Miss Tatchell, now her customary smart and good-looking self, posed for pictures as soon as Susan Blakeney arrived with her camera.

The full publicity broke not that afternoon or evening but the next day. Half way through a morning when Satan had barked himself hoarse at the constant stream of pressmen and television crews calling at the bungalow Beckworth's telephone rang. It was Miss Tatchell.

"Jesus!" she exclaimed, "I'm cheesed off with this, Len. The house is under siege. I'm clearing out for a day or two."

Beckworth laughed.

"This is where we came in, Tatch. Tell you what. Suppose I come with you?"

"I'd like that, Len, very much," she said.

THE END

A GENTEEL LITTLE MURDER
by Philip Daniels

Gilbert had a long-cherished plan to murder his wife. When the polished Edward entered the scene Gilbert's attitude was suddenly changed.

DEATH AT THE WEDDING
by Madelaine Duke

Dr. Norah North's search for a killer takes her from a wedding to a private hospital. She deals with the nastiest kind of criminal—the blackmailer and rapist!

MURDER FIRST CLASS
by Ron Ellis

A new type of criminal announces his intention of personally restoring the death penalty in England. Will Detective Chief Inspector Glass find the Post Office robbers before the Executioner gets to them?

A FOOT IN THE GRAVE
by Bruce Marshall

About to be imprisoned and tortured for the death of his wife in Buenos Aires, John Smith escapes, only to become involved in an aeroplane hi-jacking.

DEAD TROUBLE
by Martin Carroll

A little matter of trespassing brought Jennifer Denning more than she bargained for. She was totally unprepared and ill-equipped for the violence which was to lie in her path.

HOURS TO KILL
by Ursula Curtiss

Margaret went to New Mexico to look after her sick sister's rented house and felt a sharp edge of fear when the absent landlady arrived. Her fears deepened into panic after she found the bloodstains on the porch.

THE DEATH OF ABBE DIDIER
by Richard Grayson

Inspector Gautier of the Sûreté investigates three crimes which are strangely connected —the murder of a vicar, the theft of a diamond necklace and the murder of Pontana's valet.

NIGHTMARE TIME
by Hugh Pentecost

Have the missing major and his wife met with foul play somewhere in the Beaumont Hotel, or is their disappearance a carefully planned step in an act of treason?

BLOOD WILL OUT
by Margaret Carr

Why was the manor house so oddly familiar to Elinor Howard? Who would have guessed that a Sunday School outing could lead to murder?

THE DRACULA MURDERS
by Philip Daniels
The Horror Ball was interrupted by a spectral figure who warned the merrymakers they were tampering with the unknown. Then a girl was ritualistically murdered on the golf course.

THE LADIES OF LAMBTON GREEN
by Liza Shepherd
Why did murdered Robin Colquhoun's picture pose such a threat to the ladies of Lambton Green?

CARNABY AND THE GAOLBREAKERS
by Peter N. Walker
Detective Sergeant James Aloysius Carnaby-King is sent to prison as bait. When he joins in an escape he is thrown headfirst into a vicious murder hunt.

VICIOUS CIRCLE
by Alan Evans
Crawford finds himself on the run and hunted in a strange land, wanting only to find his son but prepared to pay any cost.

MUD IN HIS EYE
by Gerald Hammond
The harbourmaster's body is found mangled beneath Major Smyle's yacht. What is the sinister significance of the illicit oysters?

THE SCAVENGERS
by Bill Knox
Among the masses of struggling fish in the *Tecta*'s nets was a larger, darker, ominously motionless form . . . the body of a skin diver.

DEATH IN ARCADY
by Stella Phillips
Detective Inspector Matthew Furnival works unofficially with the local police when a brutal murder takes place in a caravan camp.

STORM CENTRE
by Douglas Clark
Detective Chief Superintendent Masters, temporarily lecturing in a police staff college, finds there's more to the job than a few weeks' relaxation in a rural setting. He soon gets involved in a local police problem.

THE MANUSCRIPT MURDERS
by Roy Harley Lewis
Antiquarian bookseller Matthew Coll, acquires a rare 16th century manuscript. But when the Dutch professor who had discovered the journal is murdered, Coll begins to doubt its authenticity.

SHARENDEL
by Margaret Carr
Ruth had loved Aunt Cass. She didn't want all that money. And she didn't want Aunt Cass to die. But at Sharendel things looked different. She began to wonder if she had a split personality.

MURDER TO BURN
by Laurie Mantell

Sergeants Steven Arrow and Lance Brendon, of the New Zealand police force, come upon a woman's body floating in the water. When the dead woman is finally identified the police begin to realise that they are investigating a fascinatingly complex fraud.

YOU CAN HELP ME
by Maisie Birmingham

Whilst running the Citizens' Advice Bureau, Kate Weatherley is attacked with no apparent motive. Then the body of one of her clients is found in her room.

DAGGERS DRAWN
by Margaret Carr

Stacey Manston was the kind of girl who could take most things in her stride, but three murders were something different – especially as she had the motive and opportunity to kill them all . . .